Marie

In the Shadow of the Lion

A Humanitarian Novel

Jerry Piasecki

Illustrated and designed by Felicity O. Yost
Graphic Design Unit
Department of Public Information

United Nations
Office for the Coordination of Humanitarian Affairs

United Nations Publication
E-00-IV-9

ISBN 92-1-130210-2

THE SECRETARY-GENERAL

FOREWORD

MARIE - IN THE SHADOW OF THE LION

Dear Friend,

The book you are about to read is a work of fiction, but the story it tells is true. What happens to Marie happens to far too many young people who are caught up in conflicts destroying their communities and their countries. It happens every day of the year. It can happen anywhere in the world.

Marie's story may upset and even alarm you. But this is as it should be. It is right to be shocked when brutal things happen to innocent people. We must use our sense of outrage to stop them happening.

You, as one of the leaders of tomorrow, have the power to change things. The choices will be yours. I hope that your generation will be the first to stand united against evil, injustice, hatred and indifference and say in one voice: no more and never again.

Kofi A. Annan

*If you don't deal with the holes
the ants make in your floor,
soon you have holes big enough for rats,
who will destroy your property.
If you don't deal with the holes the rats make,
soon you have holes big enough for snakes,
who will take your life.*

African mother

CHAPTER 7

Marie Ngonga was almost 13 years old. Her birthday was only a month away, a fact she reminded her friends of daily. This morning, however, Marie was busy with other matters. She carefully drew a circle in the dirt near the door to the small cinderblock building that served as her school, and when needed a shelter for villagers when rockets or rounds of artillery fell nearby. She could tell the difference between the two sounds they made before they landed and exploded. All of her friends could.

"Now watch carefully," she told her fellow students, who ranged in age from 5 to 15. Marie took the sharp stick she had used to carve the circle in the dust and dug two little holes next to each other toward the top of the circle and a crooked little line near the bottom.

"Who am I drawing?" Marie asked.

"How should we know?" Joseph, a 14 year old boy who was Marie's best friend laughed and teased. "You are the worst drawer in the village."

"I am not," Marie protested.

"Agnes's dog can draw better."

"That's not true," Agnes, Marie's other best friend said.

"Thank you." Marie folded her arms and stuck out her tongue at Joseph.

"He can draw much better!" Agnes laughed, as did everyone else, including Marie.

"Ok, fine," Joseph finally said, examining the circle with the holes for eyes and the crooked line mouth closely. "If you want us to guess, give us a hint."

"A hint? Yes of course." Marie picked up the biggest, pointiest, ugliest and dirtiest rock she could find and plopped it into the center of the circle.

"Mr. Alazzar!" all of the students shouted and laughed. The new nose made the picture perfect.

"What is it?" Mr. Alazzar, their teacher, appeared nose first in the schoolhouse door. Everyone froze in fear.

"Ah, nothing, sir," Marie finally said. "We were just calling to see if it was time to come back for more lessons."

"Hmmm," Mr. Alazzar hmmed as only he could. "In fact it is. Right now!"

The students started to walk toward the building. Before joining them, Marie took her stick and quickly drew two big horns on the top of the circle.

"Miss Marie, would you be so kind as to honor us by joining us in class this morning?" Mr. Alazzar shouted as he approached her from the building. "What are you drawing anyway?"

Marie quickly kicked dirt over her drawing and ran to catch up with the rest. "I was just practicing my math."

"Good. Then you can lead the class in our next lesson. Hurry!" Mr. Alazzar turned and walked quickly back into the building.

"Do you think Mr. Alazzar looks more like a goat, or a chicken?" Marie caught up to Joseph. "I think I go for goat," she said very seriously while trying not to smile.

"Shh, Marie," Joseph whispered as they walked. "One day you are going to get us all in big trouble."

"I'm not worried," Marie said.

"And why not?"

"Because when I do, I have you to protect me." Marie gave Joseph a gentle and joking push. She didn't mean it to be, but the push was just strong enough to cause Joseph to trip over a stone and tumble to the ground. As he rolled, a cloud of light brown dust rose around him and Mr. Alazzar poked his bald head through the window.

"Mr. Joseph, must I speak with you after school again?"

"No sir! I just tripped. I am sorry, sir." Joseph remembered the painful lashing he received from Mr. Alazzar's "learning stick" when he had been caught throwing a pebble at Marie, who had just a second earlier thrown the same stone at him.

"Last week I taught you manners, must I now teach you balance as well."

Joseph jumped to his feet and brushed off his shiny blue soccer shorts and bright red T-shirt. "No more lessons needed, sir. Thank you."

"We'll see." Mr. Alazzar pulled his head back into the building while Marie burst out laughing.

"A goat,"
Marie said.

"Definitely a

goat."

"This is why
girls should be
home cooking with
their mamas at your age Marie
instead of in school causing trouble for
boys." Joseph stepped around and walked ahead of
Marie.

"My momma knows how I cook," Marie called after
him.

"So?"

"So that's why they make me come to school."

Marie was the youngest of five children in her family,
three girls and two boys. Her brothers and one sister

were already grown and had gone off to live in the big city. Her two other older sisters helped their mother with the household chores, and planned for the day when a man would pay their father a bride-price and they would start homes and families of their own.

Marie was somewhat unusual in that her dreams were different than most girls in her village. She wanted to read and loved to learn. She secretly thought that perhaps one day she could teach or maybe even write a story or a book. She could drive her parents crazy with her constant questions and practical jokes. Her mother and father loved all of their children equally, but they knew that Marie's talents might lead her down a different path from the rest.

When Joseph and his friends would let her, Marie liked to play soccer with the boys and once scored a goal on the best goalie in the area. After that, she wasn't allowed to play for months.

Marie was also a great swimmer. She and Joseph would sneak off and spend hours in the river or nearby lake. It was their secret. The boys would have called Joseph a girl and the girls would have thought Marie was crazy if they knew.

Marie was very beautiful. Her silky smooth skin was the color of creamy dark chocolate and her eyes sparkled like shining caramel stars. She kept her long hair, pulled back with the hair clips she had received on her last birthday. When Marie smiled, others would too, that is unless the other happened to be their teacher, Mr. Alazzar.

Miss Marie will now lead us in our math lesson," Mr. Alazzar said smugly. "Won't she, Miss Marie?

Marie now very much regretted her choice of excuses. She was terrible in math. Walking very slowly to the blackboard, she looked at Mr. Alazzar and smiled. He frowned and pointed to the board, upon which he had written four math problems. "Answers please, Miss Marie."

Marie hesitated.

"Now, if you don't mind," he tapped his foot.

Marie knew two of the answers and guessed on the others.

"Two right and two wrong," Mr. Alazzar, who had never been a supporter of girls over ten attending school, said with a frown. "I believe you need to spend more time practicing in the dirt."

Mr. Alazzar then marched to the board, erased the problems and replaced them with four more. "Mr. Joseph, why don't you show Miss Marie how to solve these problems."

Joseph was very good at math.

"Two right . . . and two wrong," Mr. Alazzar said after Joseph completed his work. "Very good, Mr. Joseph."

As Joseph walked back to his desk near the brown thatch partition that separated the younger students from the older ones, he winked at Marie, who mouthed the words, "Thank you."

Mr. Alazzar pulled an English book out of a cardboard box he kept against the front wall. "Now you will practice your English words. Robert will lead you."

He handed Robert, who at almost 16 was the oldest boy in the school, the book and walked around the partition to teach the younger students who were being watched by one of the mother-helpers who assisted Mr. Alazzar.

As soon as their teacher left,

Robert impersonated Mr. Alazzar by strutting around the room like a chicken

while saying words in English for his classmates to repeat.

Marie changed her mind from goat to chicken. She had to bite her hand to stop herself from laughing. Since she had been very little, Robert could always make her laugh. He was one of the smaller boys in the village, and got out of trouble with the other boys by making them laugh rather than getting into a fight. As far as Marie could remember, Robert had never been in a fight in his life.

If Robert had one flaw, it was that he could get carried away with his humor. Instead of continuing to read English words as he strutted around, Robert started to cluck.

"Robert!" Mr Alazzar shouted from the other side of the thatch. "What are you doing?"

"Ah, teaching English, sir!"

"What kind of English is that?"

"Ahh, chicken English?"

The laughter died as soon as Mr. Alazzar came storming back from the other side of the partition.

Robert was sent home. He didn't view it as too much of a punishment. In fact, he was delighted to miss the hottest part of the day when the temperature in the school room rose quickly to over 100 degrees. The tin roof collected heat, and the cinderblock walls held it in.

All of the young people in the village attended school in the same building that contained only one room. Those students under nine sat to the left of the thatch divider, those over nine sat to the right. The left side was bigger because there were 42 younger students, pretty much equally divided between boys and girls. On the right, there were 18 boys and only four girls. All of the other girls had been pulled from the school to help their mothers.

Mr. Alazzar was rarely pleasant and almost never nice. After recess, however, he seemed particularly on edge or nervous. Two men who the students didn't recognize had gone into the school almost as soon as the students had walked out for their break.

"Who are they?" Marie asked a question no one could answer. "And what do they want?"

"Only one way to find out," Joseph snuck up to the building and peeked inside. He saw Mr. Alazzar talking to the men, and then giving them some money. As soon as they were paid, the men left and Joseph ran back.

"What did you see?" Marie asked.

"I don't know," Joseph said. "Those men told him something and he gave them money. That's all."

"Why?" Marie asked.

"How do I know?" Joseph said. "If you're so interested, why don't you ask him?

"Why don't you?" Marie smirked.

"Because I want to live to be 15 if you don't mind."

Before Marie could say anything, Mr. Alazzar called everyone back into the building. After that, whenever a truck horn would blow or a car backfire, the teacher would jump and look out one of the small windows. Finally, claiming that it was too hot, he let everyone go home early. No one asked why, even though this day, while incredibly hot, was actually cooler than it had been in at least a month.

"Out, out, out, out, out!" Mr. Alazzar gestured repeatedly toward the door to rush the students along. "Go to your homes and help your mamas."

Marie and Joseph were the last to leave. As soon as they were outside Marie turned around to ask if they were going to have a test tomorrow, but Mr. Alazzar immediately closed the door. He then dropped the wooden shutters on the window.

"That's strange," Marie said.

"That's Mr. Alazzar," Joseph shrugged.

"That's true," Marie agreed. "Race you home?"

Joseph looked around to make sure none of the boys had heard Marie's challenge. Under his breath he whispered. "Ready. . . go!" He and Marie raced off in opposite directions.

Marie and Joseph's families had lived next to each other for over ten years. Their homes were identical, except for the fact that Marie's family's metal roof was red and Joseph's was blue. Their families built the homes at the same time out of cinderblocks, which they then covered with concrete. Each home contained three rooms. A large single room served as the living room, dining area and kitchen. There were two little bedrooms. One for the parents, and one for the children. The floors were dirt, but the families planned to cover them with cement within the year. The families shared a well dug by Joseph and Marie's fathers, and each had their own outhouse in the back.

The homes were on a small hill overlooking the village. There were two paths leading up, one from the left and the other from the right. Marie raced up one, Joseph the other. Each had run different routes from the school. Joseph didn't want to be seen racing a girl.

Marie ran as fast as she could up the hill. She was ahead. She would win. Half way to the top she saw Joseph's face as he tried to catch up. Marie slowed down and Joseph won, beating her to the top by no more than a meter.

"I win!" he shouted with joy.

"Some day I will beat you," Marie panted, pretending to be out of breath.

"Big claim, for a girl!"

"Maybe you're right," Marie said. "You're pretty fast. . . for a boy."

"I'm a man!"

Marie darted toward her house. "Goodbye boy boy," she laughed and ran inside.

"Man, man, man!" Joseph shouted after her.

"You know you shouldn't tease him so." Marie's mother stirred a large pot on the woodburning stove. "Men are very strange creatures, and we women must support them, make them feel strong."

"Oh, mama," Marie laughed. "That's not a man, that's Joseph."

"Someday he will be a man, and you might feel differently." Her mama tasted what was in the pot.

"Never!"

"We'll see," her mama whispered. "We'll see."

Marie's home was filled with the smell of cooking onions, potatoes, spices and chicken. Her mother and sisters were making her favorite dinner, pepper soup and rice.

"So Marie, what did you learn in your school today?" Marie's father asked as they ate. At dinner, every member of the Ngonga family had to tell about their day. "Something useful I hope?"

"She learned how to race boys," her 15 year old sister Carmella teased.

"That should be useful, yes?" Her father tried to hold back a smile.

"Not if you want to catch a husband," her 16 year old sister Roseta scolded.

"I let him win, didn't I? And anyway I don't want to catch anything, particularly not a husband."

Marie's father looked very concerned. He stared at her mother, who he had known since they were children.

"No, my love," her mother said, remembering races they had run many years before. "Of course I never let you win."

"Good," Marie's father sighed. "Good." He continued to eat.

Now it was Marie's mother's turn to hold back a smile.

After dinner, Marie would get water from the well and clean the kitchen. Then it was time for homework. If any daylight remained she would usually go play with Agnes and her other friends. This was one of Marie's favorite times of the day. But, when shadows began to appear, and twilight approached, all games and playing stopped.

Marie had to be home before dark. Everyone had to be home before dark.

CHAPTER 2

"Hurry, Marie! Hurry!" Marie's father called out to his daughter. The sun was about to set and Marie had only started up the hill. Her father stood in the doorway of their home. He watched the sun drop beneath the tree line to the west. "Marie, run!"

With no homework to do that day, Marie had visited her friend Agnes after finishing her chores. Agnes lived on the other side of the village, a good twenty minute walk from Marie's. The two friends had been discussing their favorite topic, boys, and had completely lost track of time.

Marie pumped her legs as fast as she could. Now her race was against the fast approaching night. She won, but just barely. Marie ran past her father, who took one last look into the shadows on all sides before closing and locking the lock.

Recently, her father had pounded large metal spikes into the wall on either side of the door and bent the ends upward. With the help of Marie's mother, he lifted a long heavy log from its place in the corner and put it onto the spikes, barring the door securely shut.

Carmella and Roseta locked wooden shutters over the open windows cutting off the breeze, while Marie tried to catch her breath. As dusk turned to dark her mother lit an old kerosene lamp. The village hadn't had electricity in over a year, and there were no signs that it would anytime soon.

Marie had seen the two jets fly over her village..........

on their way to drop bombs on the power plant ten miles up the river. Ten miles up was rebel territory and had been for years. Days after the bombing, an army man had told the chief of the village that the electricity helped the rebels in the area, and that it was a good thing that it had been bombed. He said not having electricity was a small sacrifice the villagers could make in the war and that they should be happy to make it.

The strong, sweet smell of the burning kerosene filled the small house. As usual the family gathered around the table before going to sleep. Sometimes they would pray, sometimes they would just talk.

"Marie," her father said very softly, very seriously. "What you just did was very dangerous."

"Father I. . . "

Her father held up his hand for her to be quiet. She knew it was not an idle gesture.

"Marie," he said calmly. "You know what could happen if you are out too close to dark."

"Father, I made it home in time."

"Barely. And what if they saw you? What if they followed you? What if you led them here? What would they have done to you, to us?"

Marie's lips started to tremble. Tears filled her eyes. She knew very well what could happen to anyone caught outside at night. She started to cry. "I am so sorry, father. I didn't mean. . . I didn't want. . . "

Her father held out his arms, and she ran to them. Marie put her head against his strong chest. He felt her tears soaking through his shirt. "Shhh, my daughter. It is fine. We're safe now. Don't be afraid. It is just a lesson you must learn. Have you learned?"

"Yes, Father. I am sorry," Marie cried.

*"Don't be sorry
my little night bird,
just be careful."*

Marie closed her eyes. Her father hadn't called her his little night bird for a very long time.

Things had been so different when Marie was very young. She remembered walking with her father, hand in hand in the night. She could still feel the way the cool night breeze had felt against her skin. She and her father would chase swarms of fireflies and try to count the stars. Marie had once sung a song while spinning in circles in the moonlight. That was the first time her father had called her his little night bird.

Back then, the night was filled with magic and mystery. Darkness would cover the village like a blanket of silence which would then be broken by what sounded like millions of crickets. Soon the drums would begin to play.

Marie wiped her tears away and smiled at the memory of her family joining others in the village to dance the dances that had been done by their ancestors since the beginning of time. She remembered laughing at her oldest brother who was rightfully considered the worst dancer in the village. He had once almost fallen into the fire when he tripped over a log that was being used as bench for children. It was the same log that now rested across their door, blocking out whatever would get in.

It seemed so long ago that Marie's father would carry her home after the dance. She would hide her face against him so that the banana trees wouldn't get her. The night was a time of spirits and imagined monsters. Now, those monsters were very real.

pop! pop! pop-pop-pop!

Marie's father dropped her to the floor while her mother and sisters dove for cover. He blew out the kerosene lamp. "Stay down," he ordered.

The room was now so black that their eyes couldn't even adjust to the darkness. With all of the shutters closed tight, there was absolutely no light for their eyes to adjust to. Marie found this to be one of the scariest things of all.

Pop!Pop-pop-pop!

The gunfire was followed by a loud explosion.

pop-pop!

The Ngongas waited for more shots. Seconds passed that seemed liked minutes. Then minutes that seemed like hours. Nothing but an eerie silence filled the darkness.

"Is it over?" Marie's mother whispered.

Her father slowly rose and walked to one of the windows. Peeking out from under the shutters he said, "I think so."

A ray of *moonlight* *filled the room.*

No one spoke above a whisper.

"Shall I light the lamp?" Marie's mother asked.

"No," her father closed the shutters. "Not tonight."

"Can we go to bed then?" Carmella asked.

"No. Tonight we sleep in here."

"Father, no!" Roseta and Marie complained loudly.

"Quiet!" their father whisper/shouted. "They might still be near. Now, do what I say."

Without another word, the girls crawled on all fours into their room and pulled their blankets from their beds. As hot as the African day can be, the night can feel almost as cold. They stayed down low. A week ago a bullet had smashed through one of the shutters in the girls' bedroom, hitting the wall just above Marie's pillow. The girls hated sleeping on the dirt floor. They were afraid of ants, rats and snakes.

Marie woke up in the middle of the night. She heard footsteps and muffled voices. Crawling to the window at the front of the house, she silently lifted the shutter and froze, paralyzed with fear. She found herself staring at a man's back. He was wearing a camouflage shirt and gunbelt. He had a black beret on his head and smelled of mud and decay.

Oh God, oh God, oh God. Marie thought as she very carefully closed the shutter without making a sound. She leaned back against the concrete wall between the door and window. She held her breath and prayed. She again heard muffled voices. They moved toward the door. She saw the doorknob slowly start to turn.

No no no no no no no!

Someone pushed against the door. Marie was about to scream, but her father had jumped up and put his hand over her mouth. He put one finger to his lips, commanding her to be silent. The person pushed against the door a second time, then a third. The lock and the log held tight. They heard someone swear and then the sound of something metal carving into the wood of the door. Finally, they heard footsteps, walking away.

The footsteps faded until they were gone. Marie's whole family held each other tightly.

*Her Father
broke
from the group
to again
peek out
from under
a shutter.*

He gasped slightly, and tried not to shake. A dozen men, all carrying guns, were walking down the hill, away from the house. In the moonlight, he could see dozens, perhaps 100 more in the village below.

"What do you see, father?" Marie asked.

He quickly turned from the window.

"Nothing my daughter. Nothing."

CHAPTER 3

PLA, the initials were hacked into the Ngonga family's front door. They stood for the People's Liberation Army, one of the rebel groups fighting against the government.

"What does it mean?" Marie asked her father as they inspected the door in the morning sunshine. No one had dared look at it until daylight.

Her father ran his hand over the letters. For a moment, Marie thought she saw a look of terror in his eyes, which he quickly hid by smiling broadly and shaking his head. "Just silliness. That's all. Boys playing soldier. Now, you go to school. Learn something useful today, ok?"

"If you insist," Marie joked.

"I do insist. Now, off you go. And no racing boys," he laughed.

In the morning sunlight, her father's smile chased away all demons and fears.

"You're right, no boys," Marie said as she started down the path. "I need more of a challenge." Marie glanced back just long enough to see that her father was again touching the letters, and that he was no longer smiling.

The morning air was crystal clear and cool. Within an hour the heat of the day would begin to take hold, but for now the freshness of dawn still prevailed. It was Marie's favorite time of the day. It was when the thick green vegetation on the hillside looked even greener, and sky the brightest of blues. The smell of grapefruit and oranges combined with the scent of countless flowers, always in bloom. To Marie, this was the real Africa. A land of unmatched splendor and beauty.

"Get out of the way, girl!" Marie had been watching a red and yellow bird circling in the blue sky and hadn't noticed that she had wandered into the dusty dirt road at the bottom of the hill. The soldier driving the jeep pressed down on the horn. The blaring sound drove away the dream.

There were five soldiers in the jeep. One stood behind a large machine gun mounted in the back. All glared at Marie as the jeep passed, looking at her from head to toe. Marie ran across the road as soon as the first jeep passed and before the second could reach her.

She hated how the soldiers had stared,

and they always stared the same way. Marie didn't stop running until she reached her school, and saw all of her classmates standing by the door.

"What's going on?" she asked, joining the group.

"We don't know," Joseph said. " Mr. Alazzar isn't here."

"Really? Maybe he's just late," Marie said.

"Mr. Alazzar?" Agnes laughed. "He might be many things, but he is never, ever late."

"He's not late; he's gone," Robert came running up to deliver the news.

"What do you mean?" Joseph asked.

"Just that," Robert said. "I heard that he left the village, and that he took all of his things with him."

"When did he do that?" a boy named Frederick asked.

"Yesterday," Robert said. "Before dark. Before the shooting."

"But why?" A girl named Anna asked. "There's been shooting before. Why did he leave this time?"

"I think I know," Marie said softly. "In fact I know I know."

"What do you know?" One of the older boys, Paul, said and laughed. "You're just a girl."

"Stop it Paul," Joseph said. "Let her talk."

"That's what girls are good at," Paul continued. "All they do is *talk,*

talk,

t a l k ,

talk,

talk,

talk."

"And what are you doing right now?" Joseph said. "Are you a girl too?"

Paul shut up and Marie told them what had happened the night before, about how she had looked out and saw the rebel in front of her house, and about what they had done to the door.

"You could smell him?" Agnes wrinkled her nose in disgust. "Ugh!"

Marie nodded. "I think they're coming back."

"If they did that to your door, you're marked." Paul said. He moved right up to Marie so that they were nose to nose. "They're coming back, alright. The PLA is gonna get you girl."

"Stop it!" Joseph pulled Paul away and pushed him to the ground. "Don't talk like that."

Joseph stood ready to fight, but Paul just smiled. "And maybe they will get you too, huh?" he said as he got up and walked away.

Everyone stood completely still and watched Paul leave. Nobody said a word until Joseph broke the silence. "Come on everyone. Why do you look so sad? Mr. Alazzar is gone. It is time to celebrate. There is no school today!"

All of the students cheered; some danced. In twos or threes everyone wandered off in different directions. Only Marie didn't move from her spot.

"Would you like to come with us to my house?" Agnes asked. She was with two other girls with whom they sometimes played.

"No, Agnes. I can't," Marie said. "I think I better go home."

"Okay," Agnes said. "But maybe you can come by later?"

"Yes. Maybe."

Soon only Marie and Joseph were left standing by the school. Marie was still shaken by what Paul had said about her family being marked, and by her deepening belief that the rebels really were coming back.

"Come on, Marie," Joseph flipped her hair, which always drove her crazy. This time she didn't react. "Don't listen to Paul. He doesn't know what he's talking about."

"They did carve PLA into the door."

"They're always carving something into some-thing, or writing something on something, or doing something to something. It's nothing."

"Do you really think so?"

"Yes, I do. Now let's have some fun. I'll race you to the river."

"I really do think I should go home."

"Of course you should, but not right away." He flipped her hair again and started to run, with Marie in fast pursuit.

Marie "almost" caught up to Joseph before they reached the river. She had to work hard not to. For his part, Joseph was delighted with yet another victory. He made only one mistake. Instead of winning gracefully, as soon as he reached the river he jumped up onto a big rock that stood at the water's edge and proclaimed his dominance.

"I am king!" He threw his arms up into the air.

Marie was six meters or so behind him. She didn't hesitate, or slow down. When she reached the rock she leapt upon it at full speed and gave Joseph a shove with all her might.

Splas

Joseph flew backward into the river.

"You are king of the fishies," Marie laughed, barely keeping her own balance on the rock.

Joseph's head poked up out of the water. "Better king of the fishies then slave of the lions."

"What does that mean?" Marie continued to laugh.

"I have no idea!" Joseph shouted as loudly as possible. He too had started to laugh as he swam to the rock. "Would you please help this king out of his kingdom?"

Joseph reached his hand up to Marie, who, without thinking of the consequences of her actions, reached down with her own. When Joseph's fingers quickly tightened around her wrists all Marie could say was, "Uh oh."

Marie's skin felt so smooth and soft to his touch, but that didn't stop Joseph from pulling hard. Both he and Marie went sprawling back into the river.

"I am going to kill you!" Marie joked and spit water.

"You cannot. This is my kingdom. I rule here!" Joseph dunked Marie under, but she came up splashing.

It was an hour later, as the two sat on the rock to let their clothes dry before going home that Marie remembered all that had occurred earlier. "Joseph, why do they do it?"

"Why do who do what?"

"Why do all of them have to fight?"

"I don't know. My father says they fight for the diamonds."

"Diamonds. Have you ever seen a diamond?"

"Of cour. . . " Joseph was about to lie, but didn't. "No."

"Me neither."

It was mid afternoon when Marie and Joseph headed back into the village. It was almost the time when school would normally be letting out. But today in the village, very little was "normal." To get home they had to pass Agnes's house. She came running out in a panic. "We're leaving," she said. "Today."

"What do you mean you're leaving?" Marie said.

"My father says the rebels are too close, that the soldiers are too close. He says we have to leave before night."

"That's silly," Joseph said.

"No no it's not. A lot of people are leaving," Agnes said. "Where have you been? Everyone's talking about the fighting. It's very very bad."

"Agnes! Come in here and prepare your things!" Agnes's father shouted from a window in their house. He looked at Marie and Joseph. "And you two, go home now!"

Marie and Joseph started to run. They raced home side by side.

CHAPTER 4

"**M**arie, the truck! " Joseph shouted and pointed as he and Marie ran toward their homes. It looked like almost everything both families owned was piled high onto the back of his uncle's old flatbed truck , which was now parked at the bottom of the hill.

At the top of the hill, Marie and Joseph separated and ran to their own homes.

"Mother! Father! What's going on?" Marie raced through the door, which stood wide open.

"Marie!" They both looked up from their packing, but did not stop.

"We were so worried about you," her mother said.

"Why didn't you come home when there was no school?" her father said while opening a little metal box in which the family kept what money it had. He pushed the few bills and coins down into his pants pocket as far as they would go.

"Joseph and I were at the river, swimming."

Marie's mother and father stopped for just a moment and looked at each other. There were rumors that the rebels were already at the river and on the way.

"Thank God you're safe." Her mother ran to Marie and hugged her tightly.

"Come, Marie." Her father picked up two baskets and motioned his head toward two others. "Help me take these down to the truck. We have to be gone by night."

"Gone? Gone where? We can't just leave."

"We have to," Marie's mother said. "Do not question. Just help your father."

"Where are Roseta and Carmella?"

Again her parents looked at each other before her father said, "They're looking for you."

"What did they tell you?" Joseph asked as he and Marie carried all that they could down the hill.

"Very little," Marie stumbled under the weight of her load, but caught herself before falling. "Just that we have to leave. What about you?"

"My father said that the PLA is coming."

"So I was right," Marie said wishing that she had been wrong.

"I guess so. He also said there's going to be a big fight."

"Where?"

"Right here."

For the next hour both families kept piling load upon load onto the truck. As she worked Marie kept looking toward the village hoping to see her sisters. She saw that her father and mother were doing the same.

"Where are they?" she asked her father as they walked back up the hill together after delivering a load to the truck.

Her father's voice cracked slightly as he answered, "I don't know."

Marie looked around the empty bedroom that she had shared with her sisters and started to cry. She remembered pillow fights, laughter, and sneaking to the door to listen to what her parents were saying when they thought their daughters were asleep.

"Come, Marie." Her father walked in. He put his arm around Marie's shoulder and directed her out of the room. "Quiet now. It is not time for tears. It is time to think and move very fast."

"But father, I am so afraid."

"Be strong, Marie," her father said. "Be strong for me."

The living room was also almost completely empty

when they walked back in. So much so in fact that there really was nothing left to carry. "Just go to the truck, Marie. We will meet your sisters there," her father said.

"I'll wait for you," she said.

"No," he said sadly and put his arm around his wife. "Your mother and I need to be alone for just a moment."

"But. . ."

"Please, Marie."

There was such overwhelming sadness in her father's voice that Marie simply turned and walked slowly out the door. Half way down the hill, she heard gunshots from somewhere on the other side of the village, perhaps near the river. It was a quick burst, like firecrackers exploding in sequence.

Marie's parents ran out of the house. They shaded their eyes with their hands against the glare of the sun and searched the horizon in the direction from which the shots had come. They both looked very worried and very, very scared.

"Go to the truck, Marie!"

Marie's father ordered when he saw that Marie had stopped and was looking back at them.

"Go now!"

Marie turned and ran down the hill.

As if the gunfire had been a signal to leave, the road quickly filled with old trucks, a few rusty cars, people on bicycles and a great many more on foot. All were walking east, away from the river. Marie knew everyone she saw, but nobody said a word of greeting or farewell.

The dust being kicked up from the road by the tires and the feet of many people hurt Marie's eyes and made her cough. Joseph's uncle picked her up and put her on the bed of the truck. He had left a very small space open on the back end, enough room for Marie and Joseph's family to huddle tightly together for the ride. Joseph was already there, along with his older sister Inez and her eight-week-old baby daughter, Mary.

Inez's husband was in the army. He had promised to come home for the birth of their child, but no one had seen or heard from him in over six months. Mary was wrapped in a sheet. Inez held her close and slowly rocked back and forth. She stared out into the distance, as always, looking for him.

"Now stay here," Joseph's uncle snapped. "Do you understand?"

Marie nodded her head, saying nothing.

"We will be leaving soon. Do not get off the truck."

Joseph's uncle sounded angry, but he too was simply scared.

"Where are your sisters?" Joseph asked as soon as his uncle walked back to the front of the truck.

"When I didn't come home, they went looking for me. They should have been back long ago."

More gunshots crackled through the air. This time they sounded closer. More people filled the road. Most were now on foot. Some pushed carts filled with their belongings. Others simply carried what they could in their arms or in bundles on their heads. A few people tried to drive a couple of head of cattle in front of them, but gave up as the gunfire got closer.

Marie saw Agnes and her family walk by. For a brief moment their eyes met. Both had the same feeling, a feeling that they would never see each other again.

Several loud explosions made everyone walk faster. Those who could, ran. Marie saw smoke rising to the west, from just outside the other end of the village. She could also see that the sun was slowly starting to set.

Marie's mother and father walked quickly up to the truck. They handed Marie a basket filled with cooked yams and rice. "Hold this. Keep it safe," her mother said as if she were talking about a treasure.

There were more gunshots. Many more. They came from several places to the west.

Joseph's father took Marie's mother by the arm. "Come, come now. Get in the truck. Hurry." He helped her squeeze into the cab of the truck with Joseph's mother and uncle.

Suddenly, the road was almost completely empty. Almost everyone was gone.

"We must go now." Joseph's father ran back to Marie's. "There's no choice. Look!"

Far down the road, perhaps a kilometer away, they could see rebel troops running from one side of the street to the other. They were going into every house. Sometimes there would be the sound of gunfire from inside. Marie watched as the rebels would throw something into some of the houses. A few seconds after they did, there would be an explosion, and fire and smoke would burst out from the windows and doors. A few of the houses were simply blown apart by the blasts.

With each passing second, the rebels were getting closer. They were now only a half kilometer away. Marie could now hear them yelling.

"If we don't get out now we will all be killed," Joseph's father pleaded. He jumped up on the back of the truck. "Come on! Come on!"

"No," Marie's father said. "You go. I'll find them and join you later."

"That's crazy." Joseph's father shouted. "You have to come now."

Marie's father ran up to the driver's side window of the cab and screamed to Joseph's uncle, "Go!"

The rebels were now less than a 1/4 kilometer away. They had spotted the truck and were running toward it.

"Go go go!"

Joseph's uncle pushed down on the accelerator and the truck started to move.

"Father no!" Marie screamed as the truck rolled slowly past her father, picking up speed and leaving him behind.

Marie's father looked away. He saw the rebels approaching. He could make out their faces.

The truck accelerated as best it could. It was a very old truck, and a very bad road.

"Father! Father!" The shouts came from up the hill.

Marie looked up to her right, toward her home. Her sisters were running down and hollering loudly.

"Stop the truck!" Marie shouted. "Stop the truck!"

Joseph's father had also seen the girls running. He climbed up over the pile of furniture and onto the roof of the cab. He frantically banged on it until his brother slowed down.

"They're coming." Joseph's father looked down through the driver's side window. He saw that Marie's mother was crying.

"They're coming?" she said with both hope and disbelief. "They're <u>all</u> coming?"

"Yes, <u>all</u>," Joseph's father said. "Even the rebels.

Keep driving. But go slow," he said to his brother before climbing back over the furniture.

"Hurry, father. Hurry!" Marie shouted.

Her father and sisters ran for the slowly moving truck. They were catching up, but the rebels were too.

Joseph's father told his son to climb to the roof of the cab and get ready to tell his uncle to go fast once everyone was on the truck.

Marie's father ran behind his daughters, trying to shield them from the rebels who were giving chase. He heard popping sounds and felt something whizzing by to his left. The rebels were shooting as they ran.

"Run faster! Faster!" He shouted, hearing more pops and seeing little puffs of dirt kick up in the road in front of them where the bullets hit. "Get to the truck!"

Roseta was the first to reach the rear of the truck. She held out both of her hands. Joseph's father grabbed them and roughly yanked her up. Marie caught her sister before she could lose her balance and fall off. Carmella was next. This time both Marie and Roseta caught her, sending all three falling against the furniture.

Now only Marie's father remained on the road. He ran as fast as he could. Something burning hot streaked by his face. He felt the skin on his right cheek opening, but he kept running.

The rebels were only 50 meters back when Mr. Ngongo caught up to the truck. He jumped and grabbed onto the back. Joseph's father reached down and pulled him up by his belt. "Now, Joseph! Now!" he shouted.

Joseph looked down into the cab! "Go Uncle go!" He fell back into the furniture as his uncle pushed the accelerator pedal to the floor. The old truck groaned and complained bitterly about the abuse, but kept going, leaving the rebels behind.

CHAPTER 5

"Father, you're bleeding!" Marie shouted over the noise of the truck's engine. Blood flowed lightly down the right side of his face. The bullet had barely grazed his cheek just below the bone. She found a towel in one of the baskets. "Here father. Hold this on it."

"It's nothing," her father looked at his three daughters as if he were convincing himself that they were all really there, and safe. "Hold on," he said bluntly. "The road is very rough."

The girls smiled, knowing that this was their father's way of saying that he loved them.

The village was now well behind them and growing smaller. When the truck went over a small hill it disappeared entirely.

Now all Marie could see were the columns of black smoke rising from what had been her home.

"What happened to you?" Marie asked her sisters. She saw that their legs were covered with scratches, cuts and insect bites. "Look at your legs!"

"We were looking for you by the river," Carmella said.

"Then the rebels came and we ran into the bush," Roseta added. "We had to circle through the jungle so they wouldn't catch us."

What started as a low rumble quickly grew to a shrieking roar as three government jets flew in low, directly over the truck. Within moments there was a series of deafening explosions. The ground shook, almost knocking the truck off the road. Now more, even larger plumes of smoke rose from the village. Marie turned away as the sun dropped below the smoke-filled horizon.

At the top of the next hill, the truck came to a sudden stop, throwing those in the back tumbling against the furniture. "What happened?" Marie said, pulling herself to her feet in the growing darkness.

Both her and Joseph's fathers jumped down onto the road. They walked to the front of the truck. "Wait here!" they both said.

"Let's see what's going on," Joseph said.

"We have to stay on the truck," Marie said.

"Sure, no problem." Joseph started to climb.

Marie followed. She caught up to Joseph at the top of the furniture. She looked down at the hillside below. "Oh my."

Joseph nodded.

The truck was on a high hill. Below them they saw all of the people from the village who had left earlier. They were all lined up on the road. Marie and Joseph saw the government troops, lots of them.

"Look at all those soldiers," Joseph said loudly. "There must be hundreds of them."

"What are they doing?"

"I'm not sure."

The soldiers were moving from one group of villagers to another, but in the soft twilight it was hard to make out exactly what was happening down below.

Marie and Joseph's fathers stood in front of the truck watching, also trying to determine what was happening

39

and what they should do. Finally, they walked back to the cab. Marie's father went to the right passenger window where her mother sat. Joseph's father leaned into the driver's side, where his uncle was behind the wheel.

Marie and Joseph stared at the scene before them. No one noticed that Inez had left the truck with baby Mary in her arms. Inez walked quickly, also never taking her eyes off the soldiers.

More jets streaked overhead. They were high enough for the just-set sun to still reflect off the bottom of their wings.

"Look at all those bombs," Joseph pointed to the rows of bombs and rockets glistening in the day's final rays of sunlight. "Someone's going to die for sure."

When they looked back, Marie and Joseph saw Inez going down the road. She was already 20 meters from the trucks and was walking very fast.

"It's Inez," Marie said. "And she's got Mary with her."

"Inez, stop!" Joseph shouted.

Both fathers pulled their heads from the truck. "What about Inez?" Joseph's father asked.

"She's going to the soldiers!"

By the time the fathers looked, Inez was twice as far down the hill, and the soldiers were on their way up.

The army jeep reached Inez and didn't even slow down. It sped past her, heading straight for the truck. With the rebels behind them, there was no place for the families to go.

Joseph's uncle came out of the cab while Marie's father ordered his daughters and Joseph to get in.

"I don't want to go with the women," Joseph protested. "I am a man."

"Then be a man and follow your orders," Joseph's father snapped. "Now."

Joseph squeezed into the cab with the three girls and two women. "This is stupid," Joseph complained.

Joseph's mother looked at him. With her eyes filled with love she simply said, "Shut up."

When the jeep pulled up to the truck four soldiers jumped out. One stayed in place. He stood behind a big machine gun that he pointed directly at the truck.

"Everyone out of the truck. Now!" the lead soldier ordered. When the truck doors didn't open, he fired a long burst from his gun into the air. He then held it against Joseph's uncle's head. "Tell them!"

Joseph and Marie's fathers both motioned for their families to come out. Joseph was the last to step from the cab.

When they saw Joseph, all of the soldiers lifted their guns. One of them pushed him, face down, to the ground. "Why are you hiding among women? Are you a rebel?" He knelt in the middle of Joseph's back. "Are you?"

"Stop!" Joseph's father tried to run to his son, but one of the other soldiers blocked his way.

"Why should we stop?" The lead soldier casually walked up to Joseph's father. He stood in front of him, smiling. "Why?"

"Because we're from the village. The rebels drove us out."

"How do we know you're telling the truth? Hmm?"

The soldier on Joseph pushed his knee harder into his back. Joseph tried not to, but he gasped in pain.

"Please let him go, it is the truth," Joseph's mother pleaded.

"If that is so," the soldier looked first at Joseph's mother, then back at his father, "then you know that truth is a very valuable thing. Do you know this value? Or, are you lying?"

The soldier lifted his knee from Joseph's back only to drop it down again with all of his weight. Joseph screamed out as the pain seared through his body.

"Here." His father reached into his pocket and took all of the money his family had. "Take it. Just leave him alone."

The soldier counted the money and motioned to the other to release Joseph. He then looked at Marie and her sisters. "Girls can be rebels also."

Marie's father carefully removed the few bills and coins he had so carefully put in his pocket an hour earlier. He handed it all to the soldier without a word.

"This is all you have?" the soldier shook his head.

"Yes."

The soldier looked into Marie's father's eyes for several seconds. He made his decision. "Ok. Go down the hill. Join the others."

The two families started to walk back toward the truck.

"What are you doing?" The soldier asked. "The others are that way." He pointed down the hill.

"But our truck." Marie's father said.

The four soldiers on the ground moved between the family and the truck. The one still on the Jeep turned the machine gun on the families.

"What truck?" the lead soldier laughed. "I don't see a truck. Do you see a truck?" he asked his fellow soldiers.

They also laughed and shook their heads, "No."

"But you can't just. . . "

"I tire of this," the lead soldier said. "Join the others, or die. I don't care which you choose, but choose now." He and the others pointed their weapons.

The families started walking down the hill. They walked as quickly as possible, just in case the soldiers changed their minds about giving them a choice. When they reached the bottom Joseph's father said to Marie's, "My brother and I have to find Inez. I think she went this way." The road split in two directions. He pointed to a large group of soldiers on the left. "Take my wife and Joseph with you."

"Father," Joseph said very seriously. "Let me help."

The father looked at his son and nodded. He then turned to his wife. "We'll find you soon."

Joseph, his father and his uncle walked to the left. Marie and the others walked to the right.

When Inez had heard Joseph say, "Look at all the soldiers," she had smiled. Her husband had to be among them. He just had to be. He had finally come back. She finally found him. She knew it.

Inez saw the jeep coming up the hill and driving by. It missed her by inches, but none of the men inside were her husband so she barely noticed. She just kept walking until she reached the bottom. The road to the right held many people and some soldiers. There were more soldiers to the left, so that is the way she went.

"Did you see my husband?" she asked the first soldier. When he didn't respond, she asked the next and the next and next. Some of them laughed, or taunted her.

"I'm your husband!" a stranger in an army uniform said coming up close to her right.

"No, I'm your husband!" Another unknown soldier walked behind her.

"I am."

"No, I am."

Now Inez was surrounded.

"Please," she pleaded with her captors. "Did you see my husband?"

"What do you have in that rag you're carrying?" the man in front of her said. "Hmm? What?" He reached for the sheet holding baby Mary.

Inez had covered Mary completely to hide her from the soldiers and she hadn't even cried. Inez turned away. "No, leave me alone. Just tell me if you saw my husband."

"He asked you what was in the rag?" another soldier said. "Let's see."

The soldier grabbed the sheet. He reached in and pulled Mary out by one of her legs. Now Mary shrieked and wiggled in the air. Without a thought, the soldier tossed baby Mary to the side of the road. She hit some rocks, and didn't move.

"No!" Inez screamed and broke through the soldiers. She ran to her still baby and held her to her chest.

The soldiers smirked and walked away. One of them tucked the sheet into his pocket. He could use it to clean his gun.

When night fell, the soldiers left. They took almost everything the villagers had tried to save. Marie's father built a fire, so they could rest before moving on. It was far too dangerous to stay where they were. Joseph's mother kept searching the darkness for her family.

"I am sorry that we have no food for me to cook," Marie's mother said to her daughters. "Perhaps in the morning we will find something to eat."

"Maybe we won't have to wait that long," Marie smiled her I've got a secret smile.

"What do you mean?" her father asked.

Marie whispered something in her father's ear.

"You're joking? You did that?"

Marie nodded.

"Smart girl. Come with me."

Marie and her father walked back up the hill. When they got there the truck was gone. The soldiers had taken everything except for an old pot with a broken handle and a rag doll that had been handed down from sister to sister to sister. Marie knelt and picked it up carefully, as if she were handling a fragile memory. She hugged the doll to her chest as she had done since she was a baby.

"Where is it?" her father asked.

Mary jumped to her feet and pointed to a tangle of bushes that sat next to the road. "In there."

"Good."

Her father disappeared into the bushes. A minute later he walked back out, carrying a basket filled with yams. Marie had remembered how important her mother had said the yams were, so when the soldiers were coming, she had tossed the basket into the bushes before getting into the cab of the truck. Her father touched her shoulder. "Very smart girl."

There was a small stream running down the hill. Marie filled the pot with water, and her father carried the basket. A short while later they were all eating boiled yams, which tasted like a feast fit for a king, or a family.

When they were done eating, Carmella got up and stretched her arms above her head.

She started to walk away from the fire.

"Don't go far," her father ordered.

"Just a few steps, father," Carmella promised. "I just need to move my legs."

As soon as she left the fire's light, something caught her eye, a shadow, something moving. "Someone's coming." Carmella ran back to the fire. "Over there! Look!"

A lone figure approached through the darkness. A moment later they could hear the sound of a baby crying.

Joseph's mother ran to meet her daughter and granddaughter. Inez held her hand over the wound on baby Mary's head to stop the bleeding. As soon as they entered the light around the campfire, Marie could see that baby Mary was naked, and badly bruised. It looked as though her right arm might be broken.

Joseph and Marie's mothers took the baby from Inez, who sat down and stared into the fire.

"Your shirt," Marie's mother said to her father. "Take off your shirt."

Marie's father knew what she wanted. He quickly pulled his T-shirt over his head and tore it into strips. The women wrapped two of the strips around baby Mary's head as a bandage. The white cloth stained red where it bulged forward under the huge welt on the baby's forehead.

Marie's mother found two small, but sturdy sticks, which she held next to the baby's arm, while Joseph's mother tied them tightly in place.

Did you see your father, or Joseph, or your uncle?" Joseph's mother called to Inez.

When she didn't respond, Joseph's mother screamed. "Did you see them?"

In the firelight Marie saw Inez shake her head, no.

CHAPTER

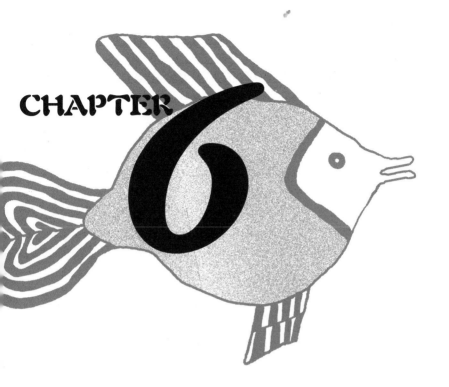

"I won't go without them!" Joseph's mother sat down next to the fire. She used a stick to push the burning wood, which made the fire glow brighter and sent orange sparks floating up into the night sky. "I won't."

"We must go. And, we must go now!" Marie's father said.

All of those on the road had started to move. Despite the darkness, everyone knew they were far too close to the rebels to stay where they were. Most of the people had already left.

"I can not go without my husband. Without my son."

"Your husband would make you go. So would your son."

"I don't care."

"Girls," Marie's mother turned to her daughters. "Take Inez and the baby and start walking. Just follow the road. We will be right behind you."

When no one moved, their father said, "Do as you are told."

The words were spoken softly, but with an intensity that ended all discussion. Roseta carried baby Mary, while Marie and Carmella helped Inez to her feet. Each held one of her elbows as they started moving down the road. They could hear Marie's parents arguing loudly with Joseph's mother. The further they walked the more the words faded until the girls could no longer hear what was being said.

Marie thought of Joseph. She was sure he would be alright. Nothing could happen to Joseph. He had always been there. "He just got lost, that's all," she said out loud.

"What?" Carmella asked.

"I said that Joseph probably just got lost." Marie tried to laugh. "You know how he would always get lost. Right?"

Carmella had never known Joseph to get lost, but still she answered with a forced smile. "Right."

About ten minutes later, Marie's parents caught up with their daughters. When they did, they were alone.

To Marie, this was the darkest night of her life. The family kept walking. They ate nothing and drank only twice when they came across small streams. For an hour Marie's father carried her on his back. With her arms wrapped around his neck he held her legs in both arms. She would occasionally doze off against his shoulder. Marie woke up often. Her dreams wouldn't let her sleep.

The people of the village walked through the night. They had all heard of a camp just across the border where they could stay, hopefully safe from both the rebels who wanted to free them and the soldiers who were supposed to protect them.

The white dots spread along the riverbank until they disappeared around a bend to the left and into a thick jungle to the right. If you looked closely you could see that some of the dots were old tents, while most were just large sheets of plastic hung on poles made from tree branches. There had to be hundreds of these plastic shelters, perhaps thousands. People were coming out of some. Marie could see that many other people were sleeping on the ground and starting to rise.

It was just after dawn that the Ngonga family stood on the top of a high ridge overlooking the border, which was marked by a shallow, muddy river. Below, other villagers were already wading across. Hundreds of rusting old cars and trucks stood abandoned near the water's edge where their owners had left them before walking through the sometimes waist-deep water. Luckily this was the dry season. If it had been the rainy season, the entire camp would probably have been under water.

"Is that where we're going, Father?" Marie asked.

"Yes." He started to walk down the road toward the river. Everyone followed.

"Ugghhhhh!" Marie's face curled up wherever the skin could curl as soon as she stepped into the water. Looking at her sisters, she saw that their faces were equally distorted with disgust.

"Just walk," their father said. "And breathe only through your mouths."

The air over the river stank and the water felt thick with mud, and raw sewage.

The water got deeper and deeper until they reached the middle of the river.

It was now at Marie's waist, and at her father's hips.

Carmella was on Marie's right and Roseta's left. She complained loudly and continuously about the stench and stuff floating by. "It's terrible! I can't do this! I can't walk in this!"

"Can you do one thing?" Roseta asked.

"What?"

"Be quiet?"

Marie had to smile, which was a mistake because

when she did she accidentally took a breath through her nose and almost passed out.

"No I can not be quiet!" Carmella complained. "This water is filled with. . ."

Who knows whether it was a native or nature who thought it would be funny to have a single hole, about four feet deep, cut into the bottom of a river. Carmella found it, stepped in it, and went straight down, disappearing under the water with her mouth wide open. She surfaced a moment later, spitting something that only vaguely resembled water from her mouth. Marie started to laugh, so did Roseta.

The second half of the journey through the river took much less time than the first, with Carmella chasing her sisters all the way to the other side.

When their parents finally made it across, Carmella was busily running after Marie, trying to touch her with her sopping wet and sticky hair.

"Stop this foolishness," their father said sternly, while trying not to laugh.

The riverbank next to the camp was quickly filling with people from the village. No one knew where to go, or what to do. The Army had set up the camp, and wouldn't let any outside people, like the United Nations, come in to help or to deliver food. They claimed it was too dangerous, and that they would deliver supplies to the camp. Some they did; most they did not.

The Army had given the people the sheets of plastic to use as shelter and would sometimes bring in bags of rice and flat bread. But the soldiers would only stay long enough to unload the truck, and search the camp for rebels

"Ngonga!" a familiar voice rang out. It was Paul Melanga, one of Marie's father's best friends from when he was boy. Paul was two years older and had always considered Marie's father his little brother. "Papa P," as Marie and her sisters had always called him, moved to a nearby village three years earlier. He and the Ngongas would visit each other as often as they could.

"You made it!" Papa P smiled broadly, walking up to Marie's bare-chested father. "It is a pity I can not say the same for your shirt."

Marie's father motioned toward Inez who was holding her bandaged baby.

The smile on Papa P's face disappeared. "I see."

"When did you get here?" Marie's father asked.

"Three days ago," Papa P answered. "This place was only half so big then. Each day it grows by so many. I came early when I heard about the rebels. It's a good thing I did."

"What should we do?" Marie's father asked.

"Come with me. The shelters are all filled. You can share ours."

"Are you sure?" Marie's mother asked.

Papa P looked at the basket now three-quarters filled with yams that Marie's mother had carried across the river on her head.

"Do you have yams?" he asked.

"Yes."

"Then I'm sure," Papa P's smile returned. "Hurry, come this way."

Papa P's wife had died giving birth to twin daughters almost 20 years earlier. He had never remarried. His daughters now had children of their own. One lived in an area firmly controlled by rebel forces. The other had moved to the capital.

Papa P led the group up a bluff and down a rough row of makeshift shelters. Toward the end they came to an impressive tent-like structure that could have been built by no one but Papa P. It was basically a large hut made of long sticks and filled in with thatch. Finally, the entire hut was covered with one of the large pieces of white plastic. Paul Melanga was long considered one of the best builders in the area.

Marie's father shook his head. "You built this in three days?"

"Oh I had help," Papa P said. "Mrs. Ndubisi, are you home?"

"Where else would I be," an elderly woman and her two grandchildren, a boy 4 and a girl 6, came out of the hut. "What can I do for you Mr. Melanga?"

"You can come meet my friends, and perhaps give them tea, ok?" Papa P turned to the Ngongas. "This is the Ngonga family. They will be staying with us."

Mrs. Ndubisi nodded a greeting and returned to the hut. Her grandchildren followed.

"She was my neighbor," Papa P said.

"And the children's parents?" Marie's mother asked.

Papa P just shook his head. There was no need to say more.

"So what shall we do now," Carmella asked.

Papa P walked up to her and sniffed the air. "Phew! I think the first order of business is for someone to have a bath."

"Not in that river," Carmella shook her head.

Papa P directed Carmella to follow the river until she was just upstream of the camp. "It's clean there, and safe during the day."

"I'll go with her," Roseta said.

"What about you?" their father asked Marie.

"If it's alright, I would like to try to find Agnes and some of the others," Marie said. She also hoped she might somehow find Joseph as well, but kept that wish to herself.

Marie's father looked at Papa P.

"It's ok," Papa P said. "Just stay in the camp."

"I will."

"And I want you back early," her father ordered.

"Yes sir," Marie said.

It didn't take Marie long to meet some of her friends from the village. She always asked the same question. "Did you see Joseph or Agnes?"

The answer was always the same "no," until she ran into Fredrick. He answered her question with one of his own. "I haven't seen them, but have you heard about Robert?"

Marie smiled at the thought of Robert strutting around the classroom clucking like a chicken. "No, but I would really like to see him. Where is he?"

"He's dead," Fredrick said softly while looking down at the ground. "The soldiers killed him on the road."

Marie couldn't believe the news that she knew was true. "But why?" she cried. "Why Robert?"

"They said he was a rebel and his family had no money to make them think any different."

Marie spent the rest of the day walking through the entire camp, searching for Joseph and Agnes. She found neither.

That evening Papa P, the Ngongas, the Ndubisis and Inez ate yams, rice and the last of the goat meat that Papa P had brought from his village. They drank tea and watched the sky turn indigo in the east and bright orange in the west. One of the men in a nearby tent started to play the drums. The family danced and sang together for the very last time.

CHAPTER 7

Papa P had given Marie's father a clean white shirt to wear. The effect against his dark skin was dramatic in the diminishing light of the setting sun.

Marie's mother thought

he looked handsome and beautiful as he danced.

It was exactly how he had looked the night their lifelong friendship turned to love. As the moon rose, its light seemed to make the shirt glow brightly, just as it had so many years before.

Marie's mother watched him dance, and marveled at how the years had taken so little toll upon his looks or his nature. He was still the boy she had raced home and the man she had married. Marie's mother walked up to him and pulled him from the dance.

"What's wrong?" he asked.

"I love you."

Marie's father looked confused. These words were very rarely spoken, although they were always felt. He looked into his wife's beautiful brown eyes and saw his own reflection in a tear.

"And I love you."

The mother and father, husband and wife, man and woman held each other until the drums stopped beating.

All at once, people started to scatter and race for their shelters.

"Ngonga, look," Papa P pointed at the river. "They're coming."

Everyone looked down at the river. They could see many black shapes moving through the water, coming toward the camp.

"They never dared come close to camp before," Papa P said. "Quick, everybody get inside. I have to find Mrs. Ndubisi. She hasn't come back from washing the pots, upstream."

"I'll go with you," Marie's father said.

"No, stay here with your wife and the children. I'll be ok. Just get inside and keep quiet."

Papa P ran down the bluff while Marie's mother and father hurried everyone inside. They kicked dirt over the fire to smother the flames before joining the children.

"Hush now, not a word." Marie's mother said as her father pulled plastic down over the entranceway and windows.

All light inside the hut was instantly consumed by darkness, which grew ever darker with every passing second. After ten minutes the sun had completely set and the blackness in the hut was near total.

"Where's my grandma?" The four year old boy suddenly burst out his question. "I want my grandma!" he whined.

"Shhh," Roseta moved to the two young children and held them in her arms. "She will be here soon," she whispered. "Very soon. But you must not make a sound if you want her to come back."

"I do. "

"Then, shhh."

"Ok."

Everyone sat in complete silence, in complete darkness. At first all they heard were men shouting and cursing in the distance. Then there was the familiar sound of gunfire. It came from near the river. A moment later there was more, this time it was closer.

"Father, the window," Marie said.

There was a strange faint orange glow that could be seen through the plastic. Over the next few minutes it became brighter and brighter, and soon filled the plastic coverings over the entrance and other windows. The inside of the hut now glowed orange.

There were footsteps running by, and more shots.

pop pop pop pop pop pop! pop pop pop pop pop

"Get down on the ground," Marie's father said. A moment later, three bullets tore through the plastic and thatch on one end of the hut and exited through the other.

"Is anyone hurt?" Marie's father whispered.

"No," everyone whispered in turn.

Marie looked up from where she lay. Two of the bullets came through the wall exactly where she had been sitting seconds earlier.

Now there was noise, lots of noise outside. Shooting, running, yelling. But, it wasn't until someone very close screamed that baby Mary started to cry.

"Keep her quiet!" Marie's father ordered under his breath. Marie's mother crawled through the orange light to Inez. She tried to soothe the baby, but Mary just wouldn't stop crying.

Marie heard footsteps running up to the hut. They stopped just outside. In all the noise and confusion, she couldn't tell if it was one person or more.

"Paul?" Marie's father had also heard the footsteps. He moved to the doorway. "Is that you?"

"Yeah," a voice from outside whispered.

Marie's father opened the plastic. When he did he was pushed back with such force that he fell onto the ground.

Five rebel soldiers stormed into the hut. One of them fired his rifle into the ceiling. With the door open, the orange light flooded in making the inside of the hut look like it was on fire.

Marie's father jumped to his feet while everyone else huddled together in the far corner.

The rebels didn't say a word. They just started going through all of the supplies that Papa P and Mrs. Ndubisi had managed to bring from their village. Marie's father didn't move as the men dumped out two suitcases full of clothes and picked up what they wanted. Two of the rebels took all of the rice and potatoes and another grabbed all the blankets and bedding.

When the hut was almost empty, three more rebel fighters walked in. Two stood on either side of the door, the third walked to the far end of the hut. He stood next to Inez, ordering her to make baby Mary stop crying. When she didn't the man pointed his gun at baby Mary's stomach.

Inez quickly put her hand over the baby Mary's mouth to muffle her cries. She turned away from the rebel. He raised the butt of his gun toward her head, but before he could swing down, a fourth man walked into the hut. The three rebels came to attention.

This new man was wearing a camouflage shirt and gunbelt. He had a black beret on his head.

"Colonel." One of the rebel looters saluted with his right hand as he walked out. He was carrying a basket filled with the grandmother's clothes and Marie's rag doll in his left.

The Colonel looked around the hut. He stared at Marie.

Oh no, oh please God no, Marie thought, smelling the unforgettable stink of mud and decay.

Her father stepped between them. "Please sir," he said. "Stop them. They've taken everything."

The rebel Colonel scratched the back of his head. "I hope not everything. I don't think those rags and garbage are enough of a donation to the people's fight for freedom? Do you?" He had turned to his guards, who smiled and shook their heads.

"You see, they don't think so either." the Colonel smiled broadly as he spoke. " You know what I think. I think you need to give more to the cause. For your own liberation, of course."

The Colonel laughed. He pulled a pistol from his belt and pointed it at Marie's father. "Your donation please."

Marie watched as her father tried to explain. "We have nothing. The soldiers took our money. They took it all."

The Colonel pointed his gun at Marie's mother. "Are you telling me the truth? Because if you are not. . ." The Colonel jerked back his hand to make it look like he had fired a shot.

"Yes," Marie's father pleaded. "It's the truth. We have no money."

"You know what? I believe you." The Colonel put away his pistol. "What can I say? You're a lucky man. Many people are dying tonight, on my orders. But I am going to allow you to live."

"Thank you."

"But, seeing as you have no money, no diamonds. . ." the Colonel looked at Marie. "I'll take her instead."

The Colonel pointed, and the rebel near Inez grabbed Marie and started pulling her toward the door. Marie's mom tried to push him away, but the man shoved her against the wall. He picked up Marie by the waist, carrying her on his hip.

"No!"

Marie's father screamed and moved to save his daughter.

One of the other soldiers blocked his way. He calmly placed the barrel of his gun against Marie's father's head and pulled the trigger.

"Father!" Marie cried. As she was being carried out the door she saw her father's dead body fall; she heard it hit the ground.

The camp was burning. Marie's tears couldn't put out the fire. She kept struggling and screaming for her father. Finally, the rebel carrying her threw her to the ground. He pulled two pieces of rope from his pocket and tied her hands and feet together. Then he found an old oily rag in the dirt, and gagged her mouth. Marie could taste the oil, and smell the smoke from the fires that were all around her.

The rebel tossed her over his shoulder and walked back toward the river. When they were half way across, Marie lifted her head and stared back at the camp. It looked like every hut was on fire. As they reached the far bank, the fires looked like small specks of orange light against the black sky. With every step the glowing specks got smaller, like fireflies fading into the past.

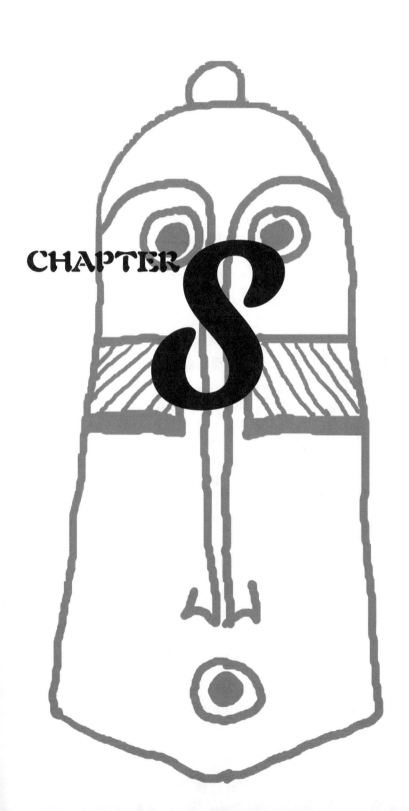

CHAPTER 8

Marie could feel the leech on her leg, but there was nothing she could do about it. Her hands and feet remained tightly bound, and she choked on the oily gag still tied around her mouth. The leech had attached itself near her ankle as she was being carried through the river. That was over an hour ago, during which time she had been passed to two other rebels who took turns carrying what she heard them call "the colonel's latest prize."

Marie couldn't see where they were taking her, but she could tell they had left the road and entered the jungle.

The smell was unmistakable

and low branches and high bushes cut into her skin as the rebels moved through the dense growth as if they were walking on a sunny street.

It wasn't long, but to Marie it seemed like a lifetime, before the sound of the rebels' footsteps changed. They now made soft, almost sticky noises as they moved in the mud. Marie knew they were going through a swamp. She closed her eyes and prayed, terrified of both her captors and the cobras that waited in the darkness. Countless mosquitos bit her bare legs, arms and face.

Perhaps another hour passed, maybe more, before the footsteps again sounded as though they were on solid ground. Marie strained to lift her head so that she was looking straight down at a beaten dirt road. The rebels moved faster now, and soon Marie heard other voices mix with the footsteps.

"What do you have there?" one man's voice asked.

"Is it for me?" Another said with a smirk in his voice.

"She's the Colonel's," one of the rebels in the group carrying Marie answered. "You know he doesn't share his new ones."

"That's why I love the old ones," a rebel laughed.

"And who knows?" another rebel said.

Suddenly, Marie felt a hand pulling her head up by her hair. She tried to scream in pain, but only gagged on the oil that slid down her throat from the rag. The rebel put his face right up against hers. His breath stank and his eyes looked dead. "Perhaps one day I will be colonel and I will have my choice of wives, eh?"

He pushed Marie's head back down until her face hit on the back of the rebel carrying her. "Anyway this one is too skinny for me."

"You will be a corpse before you are a colonel," yet another rebel voice said. Many men laughed, as if he had told a great joke, or a great truth.

Now there were lights on one side of Marie, but she couldn't look to see where they came from.

The rebels turned and kept walking. Marie heard a door being opened. She was carried inside a building and dumped onto an old couch. Her face was pressed against the back. The fabric smelled of cigar smoke and mold.

"Take care of her," one of the rebels barked out a command. "The colonel said to bring her here."

"Get out," a woman's voice snapped. "I know what to do."

Marie heard the heavy footsteps move away and the door slam. Lighter footsteps approached the couch.

Someone was untying her and removing the gag. Female hands helped her to sit up on the couch.

Marie frantically looked around the room. The gray concrete walls were pockmarked with bullet holes. Above the door Marie saw the words, PLA Embassy-home of Colonel Sam Munduba written in charcoal. The concrete floor was covered with gray and green tile. Many of the squares were broken. There was an old overstuffed chair in the corner and a wooden bench under an open window.

Marie focused for a moment on a table in the far corner of the room. It was rectangular, with four wooden kitchen chairs - one on each side. What attracted Marie's attention was the fact that it was neatly covered with a blue and white checkered tablecloth. In the center of the table was an old soup can. The label had been removed and it had been carefully polished. It held a beautiful pink flower.

"Where am I?" Marie said, never taking her eyes off the flower.

The woman sitting next to her put her arms around her. "Quiet now. Quiet."

"Where am I?" Marie screamed and tried to stand.

The woman held her down, putting her hand gently over Marie's mouth. "You must be quiet. The guards are at the door. Do you want the men to come back in? Do you?"

Marie shook her head, her eyes wide open in absolute terror. Slowly, the woman pulled her hand away.

"My name is Isabelle," the woman said. She held Marie more tightly, trying to get her to stop shaking. To Isabelle, the young girl looked like a frightened baby bird that had fallen from its nest. "I know you're scared, but try to be brave."

Marie looked up into the woman's dark brown eyes. They held no joy, but seemed kind and caring.

Isabelle appeared to be in her early twenties. Her skin was somewhat lighter than Marie's and her hair was cropped short to her head. She wore a black cotton top with no sleeves and a pair of denim shorts.

Marie started to cry. "My poor child," Isabelle whispered and stroked Marie's hair. "It's okay."

"No," Marie sobbed softly. "They killed my father."

"They kill many fathers," the woman's harsh words were spoken softly and very sadly, as if she were remembering something that had happened many years ago. *So pretty*, Isabelle thought. *So young*. "Tell me your name."

"Marie."

There were drunken shouts and hard laughter from somewhere outside.

"Hurry," Isabelle said. "Come to the bedroom. Fast!"

Isabelle half dragged Marie from the couch and to the bedroom which was through a small door near the table. Marie noticed that Isabelle walked with a slight limp, but that didn't diminish her strength, or determination. "Listen to me. Get into bed and pretend to be asleep."

Marie looked at the open window. "Let's run away. Now."

"*No*! " Isabelle said. "You must never run away. Never!"

Isabelle saw Marie still looking at the window. "Besides, there are two guards just outside. Now hurry." She took Marie by the arm and forced her onto the bed. "Stop crying, or he'll hear you. "

Marie put the end of a pillow into her mouth and nodded her head.

Isabelle pulled a light blanket up over her, leaving only Marie's face exposed. She glanced toward the living room and the sound of the approaching voice of the

Colonel. "Close your eyes. Do not open them. He must think you're asleep."

She knew she was taking an incredible risk, but there was something about Marie that reminded her of the girl she used to be. She didn't think of the danger, even though trying to save Marie could cost her her life, a life she had taken from her almost ten years ago.

"Where is she?" the drunken Colonel slammed open the door and demanded.

"Quiet, my Colonel," Isabelle moved quickly from the bedroom. "She is in my bed, asleep."

"I didn't bring her here to sleep!" The Colonel roared.

"You must wait. She is sick."

"Sick! How sick?"

"She has the fever."

The Colonel walked toward the door.

"If you go too close you will have the fever also. You could die."

The Colonel stopped. "How long?"

"Days. Maybe a week."

"I can wait," the Colonel slurred his words. "Let her help with the babies until then."

The Colonel stumbled into his own bedroom and collapsed onto the bed. The sound of his drunken snoring soon filled the house.

Isabelle took a deep breath. She crawled into bed with Marie and felt her shaking. "Calm yourself now and sleep. I will tell you all, tomorrow."

Marie couldn't talk. She felt as though she couldn't breathe. But somehow, sometime in the night, she fell into a tortured sleep, one without dreams or hope for the new day to come.

Marie didn't open her eyes when she woke up. For a long time she lay on her side with them tightly closed. She held her knees which she had pulled up to her chest.

Maybe it was all a dream, she thought. *Maybe Roseta and Carmella are in their beds, and soon mother will start yelling for us to get up and father will . . .*

Marie opened her eyes. She didn't know how long she had slept, but the day was bright and it was already very hot. She could hear a man and a woman in the other room. The man was giving orders, and the woman was promising to obey.

"By my return she will be well, no fever."

"Yes, Colonel."

Marie snuck over to the door. It was open just a crack, enough for her to see the Colonel and Isabelle standing by the table. Isabelle handed him a holster containing his pistol, which he put around his waist. He was again wearing a camouflage shirt and black beret.

"Now kiss me."

"Yes, Colonel."

Isabelle leaned forward. The Colonel grabbed her and kissed her roughly before turning and leaving the house without another word. Marie watched as Isabelle wiped her lips with the back of her hand.

Marie pushed open the door. "Where is he going?"

"To fight," Isabelle said without turning to Marie.

"When is he coming back?"

"If we are lucky, never," Isabelle said. "But then again," she turned to Marie and smiled. "Do we look lucky?"

"I want to go home. I want to go to my mother, my sisters."

"You can not."

"But he's leaving."

"It doesn't matter. They will find you. They will kill you, or worse."

"What is worse?"

Isabelle sat down at the table, and invited Marie to join her. Marie stayed standing.

"When I was first taken I was put with a group of five girls my age. Because of an escape try, they killed all of them, leaving only me alive."

"Why."

"Because I was the one who tried to escape. They made me watch and listen to them die. Then they did this."

Isabelle turned and lifted her shirt. Her back was covered with ugly scars that streaked across from her shoulders to her waist.

"And this so I couldn't run." She showed Marie where they had cut deeply into her heels and the bottoms of her feet.

"They are monsters," Marie said.

"They are what they are."

"How old were you?"

"Ten, maybe eleven. Younger than you, for sure. The Colonel let me live because he thought I was pretty. He made me his wife because I could cook. "

"I can't cook."

"But you are very very pretty. That is your curse."

"What's going to happen to me?"

"I don't know."

"Can you tell me where I am?"

Isabelle got up from the table and started toward the door. To Marie her limp seemed much more noticeable than before.

"Come," Isabelle said. "I will show you."

Marie followed.

"So why can't you cook?" Isabelle asked.

"I went to school instead to learn to read."

"Here, it is much better to know how to cook."

CHAPTER 9

"here are you going, Mama?" a boy of no more than eleven pointed his automatic weapon at Isabelle and Marie.

"Don't point that at me," Isabelle snapped.

"Siyaad points where Siyaad points." The boy jumped in front of Marie. "Siyaad kill many many soldier-boys." He pointed his gun down the street and pretended to fire.

"Pop pop pop pop pop pop

"No survivors!" Siyaad laughed.

"Let's go," Isabelle stepped around Siyaad and pulled Marie after her.

Siyaad followed.

"He's coming with us?" Marie asked.

"He's what the Colonel likes to call our bodyguard. We go nowhere alone."

"Pop pop pop!"

Siyaad pretended to shoot at a flock of birds flying overhead.

"Siyaad was wounded and can't fight yet. That's why he's here," Isabelle said.

"Wounded?" Marie asked. "But he is just a boy."

"Do not fool yourself. He would kill either one of us without a thought."

"Is he crazy?"

"Oh yes," Isabelle said.

"He's too young to be so crazy."

"When he was seven they raided his village. They made him kill his parents with a machete. Then they took him. He had no one but the fighters."

"Pop pop pop!"

"No survivors!"

Isabelle held Marie's hand as they walked slowly down a narrow dirt road that led to the rebel camp in what had been a small village many years ago.

"Do not challenge him or the other young ones. They have no second thoughts about killing. They have no wives or children. They are afraid of nothing."

"How can that be?" Marie asked, finding it difficult to walk at Isabelle's slow pace.

She could hear Siyaad laughing behind them. Sometimes he would run up and touch Marie's back, making her jump. That made him laugh all the louder.

"They keep the young ones drugged, cocaine, brown-brown, a pill they call "bubbles" that makes their hearts beat like the fastest drum. Before battle they mix gunpowder and cane whiskey. Then they make them drink it."

"Why?"

Isabelle didn't take her eyes off the road. "So they will kill and not stop killing until everyone is dead. Most don't even remember what they do."

The three turned the corner. They were now on the main road of the camp, which was so overgrown with plants and grass that it looked more like a dirt path than an actual road. It was lined with small, one-story concrete buildings, many of which had been destroyed by grenades, all of which were scarred with bullet holes and burn marks. As they passed, Marie saw that the jungle was starting to reclaim the worst of the buildings, the ones even the rebels couldn't use.

"This was once a village," Isabelle said. "I had friends here when I was little. My parents would sometimes bring me here to play but then. . ." Isabelle didn't finish her thought; she just kept walking.

The road, which was well under a half kilometer long, was mostly deserted. The three passed one group of five men standing outside of a building drinking beer. Their weapons were lined up against the wall and they waved happily to Siyaad, and whistled and gestured at Marie and Isabelle.

"That is where they go to drink," Isabelle said, still looking straight ahead.

Marie saw a group of boys Siyaad's age being led into another building, one with the words

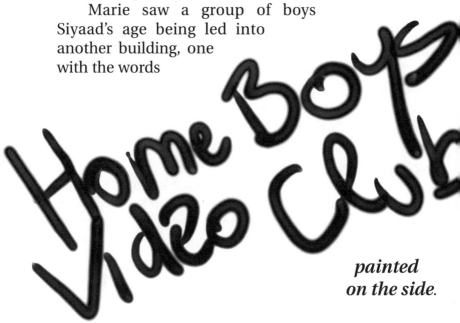

painted on the side.

It had a poster with the word "Stallone" written in big letters across the top, and a picture of the actor firing a large gun underneath.

"I am Rambo!" Siyaad danced in front of Marie and Isabelle. "Siyaad kills like Rambo!"

Siyaad pointed his gun in the air and fired a volley of shots. Marie screamed. Men and boys emerged from several buildings with their weapons, ready to shoot.

"Uh oh," Siyaad called out happily. "Siyaad slipped, that's all, no problem."

The rebels calmly returned to what they were doing. Siyaad "slipping" with his gun was nothing new.

"They make the newcomers watch that stupid Rambo movie over and over and over, until they believe it," Isabelle said softly. "Again, the drugs do half the work."

"You better shut your mouth about Rambo, mama," Siyaad jumped in front of Isabelle. "I don't need no drugs to kill you for your freedom. Because who am I mama?"

Siyaad pointed his gun at Isabelle. His voice became completely calm, his eyes void of life. "Who is Siyaad, mama?"

"Siyaad is Rambo," Isabelle said without emotion.

"Oh yeah! That is right! I am!" Siyaad smiled broadly and danced back behind Marie and Isabelle, allowing them to walk ahead.

It didn't take them long to reach the other end of the road. Once there, they stopped in front of a long building. All of its windows had been blown out and were now covered with sheets of rusty metal. The concrete had been painted red years before, but now that paint was badly faded and worn away in spots. Thick bushes blocked parts of the building so that all you could see was a dull pinkish background to the lush green leaves.

"We're here," Isabelle said. "This is where the girls stay during the day. This is where we work."

The first thing Marie noticed on entering the building was that it had no roof. The green tops of trees could be seen over the four walls, and served almost like a frame for the blue sky and white puffy clouds overhead. The building was big, perhaps as long as a soccer field, if only half as wide.

The second thing that struck Maria was the sound of many crying babies and screaming children. She and Isabelle walked past at least twenty girls in a group along one wall. Each was feeding a baby what looked like a combination of rice, smashed bananas and goat's milk. Some of the girls were Marie's age; most were younger.

"Whose children are they feeding?" Marie asked.

"Their own," Isabelle answered simply. "Their own."

At the far end of the building, Marie saw a number of girls and young women doing laundry in big tubs and hanging men's clothing to dry on ropes hung from one side wall to the other.

There had to be hundreds of shirts, camouflage fatigues, pairs of socks and underwear.

Isabelle saw Marie watching. "We do their laundry, we cook their meals, we have their children and they let us live."

Someone ran into Marie's back. "Siyaad stop!" Marie shouted. She turned to find only a seven year old girl who had been running forward, but looking backward.

The girl stared up at Marie for a moment before saying, "Sorry," and running back to her friends.

"Where is Siyaad?"

"He wouldn't come in here," Isabelle said. "Why should he? We are not going anywhere."

Marie again saw that all of the windows were blocked. There was only one way in and one way out.

"And everyone here?"

"Rebel wives, rebel girlfriends, rebel women."

"Prisoners."

"Use whatever word you want. We're here, and that is that."

Looking around, Marie saw women and girls of all ages. Most were young, many were children. There were some boys, but none over the age of seven.

"Come on," Isabelle said. "It's time for you to go to school."

"School?"

"Cooking school."

Isabelle and Marie joined a group of women and girls who were busily cutting vegetables and stirring large pots over open fires.

"We will start with something simple," Isabelle said. "You can make the fufu."

"I don't know how."

Isabelle and the rest of the women laughed. "It is a very good thing most of the men are gone," she said. "You don't want to make a mistake with their fufu."

That day Marie learned to cook fufu. She pounded the cassava root into flour and then boiled it until in became a doughy mass. She also learned how to make stew with goat meat and vegetables with which the fufu would be served.

"Where do they get all this food?" Marie asked.

"What they need," Isabelle answered, "they take."

Along with cooking, by day's end Marie had also washed clothes and watched children. Every so often she would think of her family and cry. When she did, Isabelle would pull her to the side and talk to her until she stopped.

"You have electricity here," Marie was surprised when Isabelle switched on a light that evening in the Colonel's house. The night before she had been too scared to notice.

"They have two generators," Isabelle explained. "One for the Colonel's house and another for the bar and the video place."

Marie and Isabelle talked for hours that night, and every night for the next week and a half. Each spoke of their families, and what had been their dreams. During the day, Marie would work, and long for the time when her biggest worry was getting caught drawing the teacher's face in the dirt.

CHAPTER *10*

Each day seemed hotter than the one before. With no roof, the women and girls were left to the sun's mercy and their own devices. Blankets were stretched out on four poles or long boards which had been stuck into the ground. They gave the only shade, which was usually taken up by young mothers and their babies, or people sick with malaria or other diseases. So far Marie had seen the woman who was acting as a nurse leave the building three times and bring back men to carry out the body of someone who had died. Two of the times only one man was needed because the one who died was a baby. There was little medicine in the camp, and what was there was saved for the fighters.

One morning while Marie was cutting vegetables she saw a man enter the building.

"Stay here," Isabelle said. She left Marie and walked quickly to the man who said a few words before turning and walking out.

In an instant Isabelle was surrounded by women and girls. Then, they all broke away in different directions.

"What is it?" Marie asked as soon as Isabelle returned.

"It's the men," Isabelle said sadly. "They're coming back."

A rush of excitement and apprehension flowed through the building like a wave as the news traveled from one end to the other. For some it was a moment of joy and happiness, a homecoming, a reunion. For others it was a time of absolute panic and fear.

"What do I do?" Marie felt herself starting to shake. "What do I do?" she demanded an answer.

"You do as you're told," Isabelle held Marie's shoulders tightly. "Nothing more, nothing less."

"Maybe he forgot about me?"

Isabelle looked at Marie. Like herself, she knew her beautiful young friend had but two hopes. The first was that he would drink too much and pass out. The second was that he was dead. On occasion over the years Isabelle's first hope happened. She continued to pray daily for the second one to come true.

"Just cook, Marie. Cook."

As she chopped, Marie watched what became a frenzy of activity in the building. Mothers cleaned their children and prepared them to meet their fathers when they returned. Others shared combs and helped each other with their hair and clothing so that they would look pretty for their husbands.

One girl named Binta ran up to Marie carrying her 8-month-old baby.

"Isn't it wonderful?" Binta said. "My Adamu will be home soon. You will meet him, Marie. You will see how PLA men are good papas too."

Binta was 14. She had been taken from her family when she was only 18 months old and knew life only in the PLA. She had tried to convince Marie of the rightness of their cause, and that to sacrifice in the fight for freedom was noble and an honor. Marie felt sorry for her. In her view, Binta simply repeated PLA slogans as if they were facts, and had no thoughts of her own. She did, however, have to admit that Binta did seem to love her rebel husband, Adamu very, very much.

Rumors started almost as soon as the news was delivered. There was talk of a victory, and of fighters from other units joining theirs to celebrate. The women were to make them welcome. There were also the whispers of those wondering how many had been wounded, how many killed.

When the rebel fighters finally arrived an hour later, all of the girls with husbands or children ran out to greet them. "Stay here," Isabelle said to Marie. "Don't come out."

Marie watched Isabelle go through the door. She looked around at those who stayed behind. There were girls whose babies were too sick to move, and other girls who were just trying to hide.

There was the sound of several guns being fired. Then there were happy shouts and cheers. Marie knew she shouldn't, but she had to see. She pushed a wooden table up against the front wall of the building. She put a chair on top of it, and a crate on the chair.

She then carefully climbed up until she could stand on her tip toes and peek over the top.

Marie saw many rebel soldiers walking into the village. Boys no more than ten years old carried their weapons along side grown men in their twenties and thirties. The younger boys carried supplies and ammunition in baskets, or automatic weapons just captured from the enemy in their hands.

Marie watched Siyaad running from one rebel to the next wanting to hear every detail of the fight.

Marie then saw several rebels leading in a line of young boys, Marie guessed that they were between fifteen and seven years old. They were tied together by a long rope looped around their necks. They all had their arms tied behind them so tightly that their elbows were touching in the middle of their backs.

Right in front of her, the soldiers knocked all the boys to the ground. Marie looked to her right and saw the Colonel approach. He was holding the hand of a six year old boy.

The Colonel walked next to the boys on the ground.

"This is your chance to join the People's Liberation Army and become freedom fighters. If not, you can lay here in the sun until you die."

He started to walk away when one of the boys coughed out, "I will never join you."

The Colonel stopped and walked back to the boy. He lifted his head from the dirt by his hair.

"You will never join?"

"No," the word seemed to get caught in the boy's throat.

"Very good." The Colonel dropped his head. He drew his pistol from its holster and handed it to the six year old. "Kill him."

When the six year old hesitated, the Colonel pulled him over to the fallen boy, and forced him to put the gun up to the boy's head. "Pull the trigger!" he screamed.

The boy on the ground started to cry. The six year old did as he was told.

"Good boy," The Colonel laughed. "Very good boy."

Marie lowered herself onto the balls of her feet and slowly climbed down. She sat under the table for a very long time.

Binta had run outside of the village to meet her husband. Now she stood in the middle of the road holding her baby in her left arm. She was completely alone. All others had passed. What started as a moan grew slowly to a scream. Soon her throat was raw and no sound came out. But, still she screamed. In her right hand Binta held the piece of cloth that she had cut from her favorite dress. One of the rebels had given it to her as he walked by. She had given it to Adamu before he had left.

"This is good magic," she had told him. "Keep it next to your heart."

The cloth was now torn in the middle, and covered with blood.

CHAPTER *11*

T he Colonel tried to grab Marie, but she quickly stepped away, almost dropping the four bottles of beer she was carrying to his table in what the rebels called the Freedom Bar. She quickly put the beer down on the edge farthest from the Colonel and ran away from the table.

"Your little gazelle is very pretty," the commander of another PLA unit joked and slapped the Colonel on the back. "But maybe she is also too fast for an old war lion like you."

"In the end the lion always eats the gazelle," the Colonel said, never taking his eyes off Marie. He took a big sip from the whiskey bottle on the table. "She will be my new wife."

"Whatever you say," another officer laughed, and raised his bottle to salute the Colonel. "Just don't let her talk to your old ones."

On the street the rebel fighters celebrated in the light of several bonfires. American rap music blocked out the sounds of the African night while rebels drank and danced in their best Calvin Klein jeans and Nike sneakers. Younger children from the surrounding area lined the road and begged the rebels to give them even a quarter of a can of soda. They would fight madly for the prize when they did. Some of the rebels found this to be great sport. They would toss an almost empty can of Coke to the children, and bet on which one would win the battle.

Electric light from the generator spilled from the windows of the bar and video building, as if the light itself was trying to escape. Inside the bar, at least 50 men filled a space no bigger than six by six meters. Freedom Bar was nothing more than a concrete block building that was once a bicycle shop. The rebels picked it for their "bar" because it was the least damaged building on the street. Even so, the dull gray walls were heavily marked with reminders of a now long ago battle, and scarred with graffiti. *PLA* is freedom! Death to all Traitors! No survivors! God is with us - *PLA*!

There were three old tables in the room, and a torn sofa along one wall. Still, most of the men stood as they drank and bragged. A dozen girls, the ones deemed the prettiest in the camp, served them whiskey and beer. The Colonel had called together several rebel units, and he wanted everything to be perfect.

The men would touch and pull the girls onto their laps as they walked by. Sometimes one of girls would disappear with one, or more of the rebels and not return. The Colonel would simply order her replaced by the next girl on his list. Only Marie was off limits. She belonged to the Colonel and no one else.

Marie stood between the refrigerator and a concrete wall. The smoke from cigarettes, cigars and marijuana filled the room and mingled with the smell of beer, sweat and filth. The Colonel was proud of the refrigerator. He had "liberated" it from a hospital in a Government-run sector several months earlier.

Isabelle had instructed Marie on what to do that night. She was to watch the Colonel's table and make sure he and his guests didn't run out of beer or whiskey. It was the first time Marie had to face the Colonel alone. Isabelle had been told to stay away and take care of the children while the rebels celebrated with their mothers. In fact, the Colonel had told her to stay away all night.

"Isabelle, you can't leave me with him. You just can't." Marie held onto Isabelle's hand, but she pulled it away.

"There is no choice. Just try to get him very drunk," Isabelle had said before leaving Marie at the bar. "That's what I always did at these celebrations. Now, it's your turn."

Marie did as she was told. She watched the table and brought more beer and whiskey before what was there was gone. She would then return to her hiding place next to the refrigerator until it was time to do it again.

Marie didn't want to see what was happening to the other girls in the room. She tried to look only at the table. Because of that, she barely noticed when the front door opened and three young rebel soldiers walked in. She quickly glanced over, but didn't recognize any of them, until they reached the Colonel's table to deliver a message to one of the other leaders.

"Oh no," Marie whispered.

The boy closest to the Colonel was smiling broadly. It was Paul from her village. Marie saw that he had a machete in his belt, and a strange, almost insane look in his eyes. She couldn't hear what he was saying, but watched as he gestured wildly.

He then pulled out the machete and slammed it point down into the table.

All of the men laughed very hard.

Marie saw the boy next to him jump back when the machete hit the wood. He wasn't laughing. Marie focused on his face, a face she had seen so many times before.

"Joseph?" Marie shouted.

The boy slowly turned in response to the voice. He had a bandana wrapped around his shaved head and his face was blank. He wasn't wearing a shirt, and Marie saw that the letters PLA had been carved into his chest. She could tell that the now healing wounds would soon become permanent scars.

"Marie?"

The voice was unmistakable. "Joseph!"

Marie ran across the room and hugged her friend. Joseph hugged her back until he felt a fist hit hard into his kidney. At almost the same time, an arm reached around his neck from behind.

The other rebel commander had jumped up as soon as he saw Joseph and Marie touch. He yanked Joseph backward. Pulling him to the rear door of the building. There, he pushed Joseph forward and kicked him between the shoulder blades sending him flying out. The commander stepped outside and stood above Joseph who was rolling on the ground in pain.

"You can thank me for saving your life tomorrow. Now, stay away from that girl. She belongs to the Colonel. Do you understand?"

Joseph nodded and expected the man to continue his assault. Instead, the commander turned and walked back inside. He had seen the Colonel reach for his gunbelt as soon as Joseph had called out Marie's name. The last thing he needed was to lose a fighter over a girl.

Joseph crawled to a nearby palm tree and pulled himself up so that he was sitting against its trunk. He gasped for air. It would be minutes before he would feel he could breathe, longer before each breath didn't feel like someone was twisting his lungs from inside his chest. His throat felt as though it had been crushed and his lower back combined a constant ache with occasional shooting pains in his kidney and down his right leg. He had been beaten many times over the past couple of weeks. He had lost count of how many.

Joseph stared at the building. He looked through the window in hopes of seeing Marie walk by. He looked at the door, hoping she would walk through. About an hour later, she did.

Marie hadn't had time to react when the man pulled Joseph away. As he was being dragged to the door, the Colonel had grabbed her wrist with one hand and squeezed hard, almost crushing the bone inside.

"He is your boyfriend?" The Colonel sneered before the other rebel commander returned.

Marie lowered her head and stared at the floor. "No sir. I have no boyfriend."

"Oh yeah, he is her boyfriend, big time," Paul said happily.

"Quiet! " the Colonel snapped and Paul backed away.

"This one says he is your boyfriend," the Colonel looked toward Paul for just a second before locking his bloodshot eyes back on Marie.

"No, that is not true" Marie didn't look up from the floor.

"Then who is he?"

"He is just someone I knew from long ago."

"Are you lying to me?" The Colonel's words were like razors spinning through the air. He squeezed harder.

"No sir, never." Marie cried out in pain.

"Good." The Colonel released her hand with such force that Marie almost fell to the floor. "Then get us more to drink!"

As she walked back toward the refrigerator the other commander rejoined the group at the table and started to laugh. "Don't worry, Colonel," he said. "That cub will not be hunting gazelle tonight."

"You know, I should shoot him," the Colonel said as if talking about swatting a fly.

"No, don't," the other rebel commander was equally as casual. "He's going to be a good fighter. He's only been here just over a week, and he's already killed three times."

Marie overheard the conversation. She felt dizzy, but wouldn't fall. She wanted to cry, but didn't dare.

"I told you that the PLA was gonna get you girl," Paul said. He walked by Marie as if he was just going to the other side of the room and spoke through the corner of his mouth, the corner facing away from the Colonel. "Tonight they gonna get you good. Real good. Maybe I get you too."

Paul walked away and joined a group of young rebels drinking beer against the far wall.

He pointed at Marie and said something that made the rest of the rebels laugh. Marie looked away and took more whiskey to the Colonel's table.

Over the next hour Marie constantly looked for an opportunity to get outside. She knew Joseph would be there waiting. Every time she started to move toward the door, the Colonel would call her, demanding more whiskey and a kiss. Marie would bring the whiskey and run. The more the men drank, the more they laughed at the Colonel's little game. Finally, Marie saw her chance.

A fight had broken out between a thirteen year old and a sixteen year old and all of the rebels had gathered around to watch the fun. Marie cautiously walked to the door. As soon as she started to push it open, someone reached around her and jerked it shut.

"And where are you going?" the Colonel put his arm around Marie's waist and pulled her close. He reeked of whiskey and held the half-chewed tip of a cigar in his mouth.

"I was just going to the toilet."

"Yes? To the toilet? Nowhere else?"

"No sir."

The Colonel let go of Marie and grabbed a 13 year old girl named Anita Towa. Marie knew her from the woman's building. The two of them had taught three younger girls how to jump rope.

The Colonel pulled a knife from his boot and held it to Anita's throat. "If you don't come back, I will slice her open, yes?"

Anita started to tremble with fear. That made the Colonel laugh. "Your fate is in her toilet," he laughed loudly, ran the knife lightly over her skin, and kissed her noisily on the cheek.

Anita's eyes filled with tears. "Don't worry," Marie said. "I'll be back."

CHAPTER 72

"Joseph?" Marie whispered as she stepped away from the door. The noise of the celebration inside and out front still filled the night, but the only light in the back came from the moon and the stars. Marie's eyes hadn't yet adjusted to the darkness. "Joseph?"

"Over here," a voice whispered back.

Marie saw a shadowy form get up from the ground next to a palm tree.

"Over here."

Marie ran through the darkness until she ran into Joseph.

"I can't believe it's you," Marie forgot for just a moment where they were and started to shout, but the words faded quickly back into a whisper. "What happened to you back on the road? Why didn't you come back with Inez and baby Mary?"

"We were looking for them when the soldiers took us," Joseph said. "They thought we were rebels and put us on a truck. When we got to a village they took my father and uncle into a building and let me go."

"What happened to them?"

"I don't know. They wouldn't let me stay. The soldiers pointed their guns at me and told me to run. So I did. I ran back to try to find you and my mother, but that first night the PLA found me and took me."

"The PLA killed my father when they took me," Marie's eyes misted over, but she focused on her friend.

"And my mother?" Joseph asked.

Marie shook her head. "She waited for you."

"Please no," he threw his head back against the tree. "Mother, no."

"Maybe she's ok, Joseph." Marie gently touched Joseph's shoulder. "Maybe the rebels didn't come.

Maybe she's still looking for you."

"Maybe," Joseph said weakly.

"Yeah, maybe."

"And what about the others?" Joseph asked. "Your mother? Our sisters?"

"I also just don't know."

Joseph slumped back down to the ground. Marie sat next to him.

They sat in silence and looked at the stars.

The same stars that they had seen so many times before now looked different, and distant. School, play, their homes, their lives were now only memories and dreams. Now what was real was a nightmare.

"Did you kill three people?"

Joseph didn't take his eyes off his favorite star. It blinked blue, then red, then green and back to blue again. He had always wondered why. "You have to escape."

"Joseph I can't. If I do they'll. . ."

Joseph jumped up to his feet and pulled Marie after him. "Run. Run now!" He pushed her, hard. When she didn't go, he pushed her again. "Run!"

"Joseph stop!"

"Run! Before it's too late!"

He pushed so hard that Marie stumbled backwards.

"Run now!"

"Where is my new wife?" the Colonel's drunken voice boomed from inside the bar. "I want my new wife!"

He was coming out.

"Hide, Joseph." She shoved Joseph back to the tree, which he tucked behind just as the door flew open.

"There you are."

Marie moved away from the tree. The Colonel stumbled to her and picked her up with one arm and threw her onto his shoulder as if she were a sack of grain. He sang and laughed as he carried her home.

The Colonel fell twice before reaching his house. Marie felt blood trickling down her back from a cut made by a sharp stick, and a knot rising on the side of her knee where it had hit a rock. But all she could think of was

Joseph, of how he had killed and of how he had tried to make her run.

The Colonel opened his door by ramming Marie's behind into the wood. He tripped walking through, tumbling with Marie to the floor.

"Stay there," the Colonel ordered Marie as he pulled himself up by holding onto the table. "I think we need a drink."

The Colonel reached into a box at the far end of the room and pulled out a bottle of whiskey. He then took Marie by the wrist and dragged her along the floor to the bedroom. Once inside, he let go of Marie and opened the bottle. After taking a long drink he offered it to Marie who had crawled into one of the far corners of the room.

"Now you."

Marie didn't say anything, she just curled into a small ball and tried to disappear into the walls.

"I said, now you!" the Colonel screamed. He raced to Marie and put the bottle to her lips.

"No," she begged. "No."

"Drink," the Colonel pushed the bottle between Marie's lips and pulled her head back. Whiskey poured into her mouth and down her chin. Marie twisted her head free. She was choking on the burning liquid. She spit out what she could.

"Drink more!" The Colonel again moved the bottle toward Marie, but she swung her arm, knocking it out of his hand. The bottle dropped to the tile floor, shattering when it hit.

The Colonel exploded. "You little witch! Look what you've done." He hit Marie with the back of his right hand. It felt as though the whole side of her face had split open. Then he hit her with his left and the world disappeared.

The next thing Marie felt were her arms being pulled up above her head. She opened her eyes to see the Colonel lacing his belt around her wrists. She was lying on the bed and all parts of her face ached.

"What are you doing?" her mouth hurt when she talked. It felt as though several of her teeth were loose or broken.

The Colonel tightened the belt around her wrists until she felt the leather cutting into her flesh. He then tied the ends of the belt around the metal bedpost. "Making sure you're comfortable while I get more whiskey."

With one hand the Colonel squeezed Marie's cheeks so that they met inside of her mouth. The pain was excruciating. "When I get back, you will pay for what you did. Yes?" He moved his hand so that her head nodded up and down.

"Good." The Colonel let go and left.

CHAPTER 13

"**M**arie."

Marie barely heard the familiar voice whispering her name. The sound floated through the fog that filled her mind. She tried to pull free, but the belt was too tight and very well tied. She closed her eyes against the pain and started to drift away from consciousness. Then all went black.

What seemed like just a moment later, Marie felt her mother's hand stroking her hair. "Marie, wake up Marie. It's time for school."

"No, mama, no school today. There's no school today." Marie smiled and turned her head, hoping her mother would believe her and let her sleep. It had never happened, but Marie tried almost every morning.

"Marie!"

No, it wasn't her mother, it was her father calling her.

"Father, I thought they killed you." Marie mumbled into the mattress. "I love you, father. I miss you so much. I was so scared. The dream was so real. Help me, father. Please help me. I don't want to wake up. I don't want to, ok?"

"Marie!" The whisper was stronger and more insistent. "Marie!"

Marie's father's voice blended into, and then became another. Marie half opened her eyes. "Joseph?"

"Come on, hurry," Joseph climbed in through the window. He carried a knife which he used to cut the belt from the bed. He unwrapped the leather from Marie's wrists, which were deeply bruised and bleeding. Joseph remembered how smooth they had felt when he had grabbed them so that they would both fall back into the river.

King of the Fishies, that's what she had called him. Joseph pushed the memory from his mind and pulled Marie up from the bed. He made sure not to touch her wrists. "Let's go."

Marie tried to stand, but she stumbled to the floor. "I can't, Joseph." Her whole body ached. She felt so weak. She only wanted to rest, to sleep, to die.

"You have to," Joseph again pulled her up. "The Colonel will be back right away. We have to move fast."

Joseph lifted her to her feet and half carried her toward the window.

"We can't," Marie closed her eyes, and started to slump back to the floor. "The guards will stop us."

Joseph held her up. "The guards are all drunk at the celebration. There's no one. We can go, if we go now."

"But there's no place to go." Marie shook her head. She kept her eyes closed. She didn't want to see.

"Yes there is. Maybe 10 kilometers to the west there's a center for girls. I heard the soldiers talking about it before they let me go. It's where the rivers meet."

"Are you sure?"

"Yes, I'm sure." Joseph nervously looked toward the front room of the house. "That's what they said. We have to go there. Hurry, before it's too late. Be strong, Marie. Be strong for me."

For just a second, no more than a blink in time, Joseph's voice again became her father's. Marie's mind cleared. She was ready to move.

"I will be strong, father," she said softly, almost to herself. "I will be very strong."

"What did you say?" Joseph asked as he felt the strength return to his friend's body. He let go knowing that she wouldn't fall.

Suddenly the sound of men's voices and laughter came from the street. The Colonel was bringing his friends.

"Come on, Joseph," Marie said. "We have to go now."

Marie and Joseph climbed out through the window. They ran as fast as they could, racing through the brush and up a small hill behind the house. They ran faster then they had ever run before. When they reached the top they stopped to catch their breath. Looking back, they both saw the Colonel's face in the window. He was staring directly at them.

"Go go go!" Joseph shouted. As he and Marie started down the other side of the hill, they heard the sound of the bell the rebels used as an alarm ringing madly in the soft night breeze.

The land on the other side of the hill had been cleared for timber. The jungle was now at least a kilometer away. If they could make it there, if they could get deeply enough into the jungle, they had a chance.

In the camp the Colonel screamed to his troops. "One hundred American dollars to whoever finds the girl!"

Marie and Joseph ran through the tall grass. The land rose and fell in a series of small plateaus, much too small to be called hills. They couldn't see the rebels who were chasing them, but they knew they were on their way.

In the village, rebels were running in all directions. "I want the girl back alive," the Colonel yelled. "No dollars if she is not alive."

Several groups of rebels jumped into jeeps or small trucks. Two of the jeeps started driving up the small hill behind the Colonel's house.

Marie and Joseph were getting closer. The jungle was now less than a quarter of a kilometer away and the last of the run was almost all down hill.

"Keep running, Marie. Keep going!" Joseph shouted as they approached what looked like a dark wall of trees and thick undergrowth.

The jeeps made it to the top of the hill. The drivers didn't stop. Instead they pushed down on the accelerators and started blowing their horns.

When they heard the horns the tree line was only 20 meters away. By the time they reached it, they could hear the engines roaring ever closer. When Joseph and Marie pushed through a tangle of branches, Joseph stopped running.

"What are you doing?" Marie stopped a few meters ahead. "Come on, Joseph! We have to go!"

The jeeps were almost there.

"Run," Joseph said.

"Run fast Marie.

You were always the fastest, now go."

The approaching headlights lit the jungle in an eerie green light.

"We'll run together, like always" Marie said.

"No, they're too close. They'll catch us."

"I won't go without you."

"Please, Marie," Joseph begged. "Run! Go now. You have a chance if you run fast and don't stop. You have to go. They can't have us both. Not both."

Marie started to back farther into the jungle. "Come with me, Joseph. They'll kill you. You know they'll kill you."

"Don't you understand?" Joseph said without emotion. "They already did."

He turned and stepped out of the jungle before Marie could say another word. As he did, the jeeps rolled to a stop.

Marie ran. She didn't know what else to do.

Five rebels jumped out of one jeep, four out of the other. Paul was in the lead. They all carried machetes. Joseph stood still, shielding his eyes from the glare of the lights.

"Good morning, my friends!" Joseph shouted, trying to sound drunk. He couldn't help but notice the sunrise beginning in the east. He was amazed at its simple beauty, something he had never really noticed before.

"I think I had too much whiskey and got lost. Can you give me a ride back to camp? "

"Where is she? Where's Marie?" Paul screamed and waved his machete in front of Joseph. He had been in the first jeep.

"Who?" Joseph staggered.

"You helped Marie escape," Paul spit out the words. "Now you're going to pay. I told you the PLA was gonna get you too."

"Paul, Paul, Paul," Joseph shook his head. "I don't know what you're. . . "

The first machete hit Joseph just under the cheekbone, splintering his jaw. The second came down in the middle of his forehead, splitting open his skull. The rest didn't matter.

In the jungle Marie ran away from the rising sun.

Epilogue

"How long has she been here?" One of the workers at the girl's missionary center asked so that the girl they were watching couldn't hear. The girl sat on a couch on the far side of the room. For hours she had been staring out a window, as if waiting for someone who she knew would never arrive. Her eyes were dull brown, without sparkle or hope.

"She came in yesterday," the other worker said. "She hasn't said a word."

The first worker noticed that the girl's skin was badly bruised and wounded and that her hair was tangled and matted with dirt.

"Why hasn't she had a bath?"

"We tried, but when anyone touches her she starts to scream."

"Poor child, she must have gone through hell."

"Or worse."

The workers started walking away. "Well," the first one said. "At least she's alive. They could have killed her."

At the window Marie whispered ever so softly so only she and her shadows could hear, "Don't you understand? They already did."

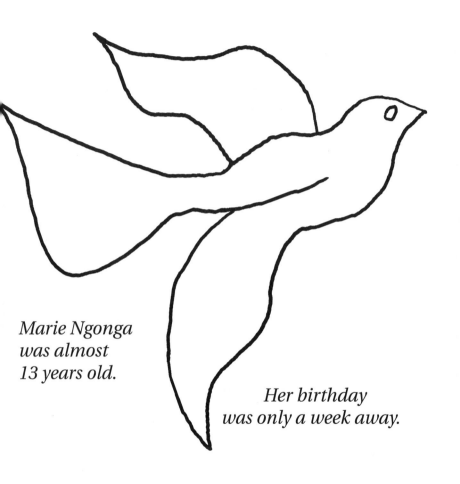

Marie Ngonga was almost 13 years old.

Her birthday was only a week away.

Your turn

If you want to, you can change the world. It's up to you.

Everything you just read, and much worse, has happened, and is happening to thousands of young people like yourself every single day of the year. It is happening right now as you read these words. It will be happening as you go to school, as you eat your dinner and as you go to sleep tonight. This is the truth.

There is a reason why this book was written. So far, no generation has been able to stop these terrible things from happening. We hope that maybe, just maybe, yours will be the first.

Many years ago, the founders of the United Nations had a vision of saving future generations from the horrors of war. They wanted to ensure that every man and woman, every girl and boy, had a chance to live in peace and freedom. That is still the goal of those of us who work at the United Nations today.

The problems we face are not easy, and the statistics are very scary. Nearly 30 million people around the world have had to escape from their own homes, like Marie, because of conflict. About two-thirds are children. Some of them have fled to other countries, while others are displaced in their own countries. Over the last ten years, two million children were killed, more than one million orphaned, and six million severely injured or permanently disabled. About 800 children are killed or maimed by landmines every month. Some

300,000 young people under the age of 18, like Joseph, are being forced to fight, kill and die as soldiers in about 30 different conflicts around the world.

These numbers represent people just like you, people who are losing their lives and everything they own. When they are sick, there is often no medicine. When they are hungry, there is often no food. And even those who do survive physically have seen, experienced or done things that leave them scarred emotionally for the rest of their lives.

The United Nations is trying to protect the innocent victims of conflict in different ways. There are a number of international agreements that Governments have endorsed. Some of these are the Geneva Conventions, the Universal Declaration of Human Rights and the Convention on the Rights of the Child. Plus, we are encouraging governments to sign new legal agreements, like the Optional Protocol to the Convention of the Rights of the Child, which raises the age limit for the forced recruitment of soldiers from age 15 to age 18. And then there's the prospect of an International Criminal Court, which will make sure that no one who commits war crimes can walk away unpunished. You can learn about all these things by logging on to the United Nations home page (www.un.org).

But we can't wait for treaties to be signed or for laws to be obeyed. We have to save lives now. This book was created within the Office for the Coordination of Humanitarian Affairs. (At the United Nations we call it OCHA). OCHA works together with other organizations in the United Nations family, like UNICEF, the Office of the High Commissioner for Refugees, and the World

Food Programme. It also works with what we call non-governmental organizations (NGOs), and the Red Cross movement to make sure that people get the life-saving support they need. Just click on "humanitarian affairs" on the UN website to find out about all of OCHA's partners and what they're doing to help. Log onto another site (www.reliefweb.int) to get in-depth updates on current emergencies.

We must all work to make sure that Marie and the millions like her are not forgotten. In 1997, United Nations Secretary-General Kofi Annan appointed a Special Representative for Children and Armed Conflict. The goal of this office is to ensure that the rights of children are protected in every conflict around the world. These efforts have now led the United Nations Security Council to recognize that the protection of children is an absolutely vital part of its mandate to maintain peace and security.

HOW CAN YOU HELP?

Actually, there are lots of ways you can help. For instance:

• You can set up a Humanitarian Club in your school where you can work on projects to help the innocent victims of war and violence;

• You can write articles in your school newspaper on these issues in order to let everyone in your school know what's really going on in the world;

• You can write to newspapers, radio and TV stations, networks, and movie studios asking that the truth about what young people are going through be told loud and clear;

- You can start up a collection and donate money to charities that are helping to save the lives of children;
- You can write or call government leaders, demanding that they support international humanitarian treaties, laws and programs; and, if nothing else,
- You can remember Marie and the many like her, so that some day when you have a choice to make. . . you'll make the right one.

There a lot of people here at the United Nations and elsewhere who want to help you help others. One great place to look is the United Nations CyberSchoolBus at www.un.org/cyberschoolbus. This exciting web site is designed to give you information on a variety of humanitarian issues. It covers areas of worldwide concern like human rights, landmines, the environment and health.

We really want to hear from you. Your reactions, thoughts, ideas and experiences are very important to us. Phyllis Lee and Jerry Piasecki worked together in the creation, development and nurturing of this book and project. Phyllis Lee is the Chief of the Advocacy Unit at OCHA and can be contacted at: leep@un.org. Jerry Piasecki can be reached at piasecki1@aol.com.

Remember, if you want to help - you can. If you want to change the world - you will.

44975—August 2000—3,180